KU-027-569

WHEN IRELAND WENT TO SPAIN
and other stories

Dublin City Libraries
Withdrawn From Stock

Children's Collection
- Irish

" And now to cross the One Man's Path!"
[*Page* 64]

When Ireland went to Spain

and other stories

by

M. GRANT CORMACK

Author of
"Animal Tales from Ireland"

illustrated by
W. F. PHILLIPS

Dublin City Libraries
Withdrawn From Stock

GEORGE G. HARRAP & CO. LTD
LONDON TORONTO WELLINGTON SYDNEY

In memory of Jet

........Iss.......... Department
Acc. 4.5.12.037.
Class..........K
Date.......26 SEP 1959
Inv   25498
S...............c   9/6
Rebound..................

Lesbspianns puiblide
Catpoc ór a   iist

EX00005212

First published in Great Britain 1959
by GEORGE G. HARRAP & CO. LTD
182 High Holborn, London, W.C.1

© *M. Grant Cormack* 1959

Composed in Bell type and printed by
Western Printing Services Ltd, Bristol
Made in Great Britain

Contents

Contents

Leabar_____ puno____
_____ _____ Clua8

1

When Ireland went to Spain

~~~~~~

It was raining and raining all over Ireland. For weeks the mountains had hidden behind grey mist until nobody was sure that they were still there at all, the waterfalls in the glens had become roaring torrents, and in the midlands the Shannon had enlarged her bounds so far as to spread great shallow sheets of water across the neighbouring counties. Every place was soaked and dripping; yet, morning after morning, when the animals woke up and looked out hopefully it was to find the rain still pouring relentlessly down. They were all thoroughly miserable. The Field-mouse had been twice washed out of her house; the lark's nest was flooded; the Badger's roof had sprung a leak, and the Rabbit's burrow was beginning to get soggy; the Horse complained of indigestion from eating wet grass, while the Sheep said her fleece was so heavy with moisture that she could hardly walk about. Then, to crown all, the swallows began to arrive and make everybody jealous by describing the fine, warm weather they had been enjoying on the Mediterranean coast.

"Sunshine every day!" exclaimed the swallows. "We didn't run into any heavy clouds until we were half-way across the English Channel. You don't mean to say it's been weather like this ever since the end of January! How on earth do you folks stand it?"

"Rain, rain, go to Spain" [sang out a little Mouse]
"And never show your face again!"

"I'm fed up with this," grumbled the Cat, who hated the wet weather more than any of the rest did. "I wish *we* could all go to Spain."

"Perhaps we can!" said the Rabbit suddenly. "Don't ask me how, folks—not yet. I have an idea, but it wants thinking out." And away he bobbed up the Torr Head road, over the crest of the hill and past the twin syca-mores that stood entwined to meet the blast, till he came to a secluded spot he called 'the blackbird's parlour.' This was a grassy oblong (the size of a small room) with a streamlet running through. In a dip below the level of the road it lay, enclosed by high hawthorn-hedges and presided over by a gnarled, wind-beaten alder whose branches spread above it in the shape of a fan. Nobody ever came there except the blackbird—and the Rabbit, when he had a problem to solve that required concen-tration.

"The grass is wet!" called the blackbird warningly, as the Rabbit arrived.

"Do you think I don't know that?" the Rabbit re-torted, as he splashed down into the blackbird's parlour. "Can you tell me anything that isn't wet this weather?"

The blackbird put his head on one side with a cheeky twinkle in his eye. "The inside of a stone?" he sug-gested, chuckling.

But the Rabbit responded with such a pained look that the bird, realizing his little joke had fallen flat, took himself off and gave his friend peace to think.

The drizzling afternoon wore on, and just before tea-time the Rabbit emerged from his retreat, simmering with his great idea. As he explained his plan that night to his ally, the Horse, it appeared quite simple.

"The reason Ireland is so damp and chilly," the Rabbit began, "is that it lies too far north, right in the

path of the wet westerly winds. Now, if we could manage to move the country farther south—say, down
opposite Spain—we'd have warm, dry weather and sunshine, just as the swallows described. Wouldn't that be
nice?"

"It would, surely," agreed the Horse, "but—shift
Ireland into another place? How could you ever do that?"

"Well, Ireland's an island, isn't it?" explained the
Rabbit patiently. "As far as I can see, the advantage of
an island is that it's not attached to anything, so you can
put it wherever you want it to be. All that's needed is a
good hard push to send us skimming over the water; but
since there's nobody to do the shoving except ourselves
the sooner we get this plan into operation the better,
before we're all dead of coughs and sneezes."

Before the week was out every animal in Ireland had
heard of the Rabbit's plan and was heading for the north.
As each contingent arrived, the Rabbit directed the
animals to their places on the north coast; when he was
sure they were all gathered and he had an unbroken line
stretching from Fair Head to Inishowen he gave the
word and they all began to push. They pushed and
pushed and pushed, every little animal straining and
striving and panting, but Ireland still remained firmly
rooted where it had always been.

"Whew!" cried the Horse, pausing for breath, his skin
glossy with perspiration. "It isn't possible, Rabbit!"

"Of course it's possible," said the Rabbit tartly.
"There must have been somebody not pushing."

"I'm sorry, Rabbit," piped the tiny voice of Lochag
Mouse. "It was me. I couldn't get in."

The Dog moved over nearer the Badger in order to
make room for Lochag, and they all got ready to heave
again. But before they started the Rabbit shouted,

"Hey, you birds, get up and fly! We can't shift Ireland with you sitting on it!"

" I'm sorry, Rabbit. . . . It was me"

When the Rabbit gave the signal for the second time the birds all rose in the air and the animals pushed and pushed, the Rabbit himself included, until, just as they were coming to their last gasp, they heard a wrenching sound beneath them, and without warning the land shot forward, riding over the waves. It happened so suddenly that some of the animals were almost caught by the inrush of the sea and had to jump quickly on to dry land before Ireland skimmed away out of their reach. Indeed, the Cat might have been drowned had it not been for the prompt action of the Horse who, hearing her shrieks, picked her up in a twinkling by the scruff of the neck and dropped her on the edge of the shore.

"Ow!" she wailed, tenderly feeling the back of her neck where the Horse's teeth had gripped her. "Ow! my eighth life gone!"

"Cease whining and shove!" shouted the Rabbit, and reluctantly the Cat went back to work.

All along the north coast the animals toiled and heaved, pushing Ireland before them, until by evening they were passing the Bay of Biscay. It was fine now and warmer already.

"Why not turn in here, Rabbit?" called the smaller birds, who were tired of flying and wanted to land.

"We can't turn," the Rabbit gasped, "not unless I send the animals all round to the west coast. We have to keep straight on."

"Tell them to leave off now," advised the swallows. "By the time the country stops moving you'll find we'll be far enough south to satisfy anyone."

The Rabbit was glad to be able to say "Stop!" not only because he and they were well-nigh exhausted, but because of his discovery that some animals had been pushing so much harder than others that the coastline was becoming indented and irregular, a thing which irked the Rabbit's tidy mind. Near where he had been in charge of operations, along the coast of Antrim and part of Derry, everything was in order, but farther west the irregularities increased, until in the extreme north-west the whole scheme had apparently gone to pieces.

While the other animals were still resting after their exertions the Rabbit set out to investigate. As he suspected, the Horse and Donkey—both hard workers—had pushed with such energy that they had forced two great bights into the land, the one at Lough Foyle and the other at Lough Swilly. "I should have placed you two farther apart," the Rabbit observed, and went on to see who was responsible for the unseemly projection of land at the north-west corner that stuck right out into the ocean. First he passed a row of little animals lying half asleep—mostly mice and shrews—and he could scarcely blame them for not pushing harder, since they had obviously done their best. No, there must be a bigger animal somewhere who had not done his share.

At long last the weary Rabbit reached the farthest extremity of land, and there, on the tip of Malin Head, whom should he find but the Cat, sitting washing her face!

"I might have known it!" the Rabbit cried wrathfully. "Take a glance at our coastline over yonder, and then look at your bit, you lazy, good-for-nothing animal! Can't you ever do a decent day's work?"

"Don't talk to me like that, Rabbit," whined the Cat sulkily. "I was nearly drowned, so I was."

"Small loss that would have been," retorted the Rabbit, who was really very angry.

"Anyway, you didn't treat me fairly," the Cat went on. "You never do. My part of Ireland was full of mountains, and they're much the heaviest things to shift, as you know very well."

"Who put you there?" demanded the Rabbit indignantly. "Not me. No, it was yourself was afraid you'd get caught by the sea again on a flat coastline. Why didn't you stay beside the Horse, where I put you?"

"He's too rough for me," mewed the Cat. "He nipped my neck."

"Oh, you—you——" muttered the exasperated Rabbit, and, not finding a word strong enough to express his feelings about the Cat, he left her and started back towards Fair Head.

As if to make up for the Cat's negligence, the Rabbit and his friends were very particular about their part of the coastline, setting the columns of rock in nice neat rows before they went to bed. You can still see the regular way the Rabbit arranged the rocks at the Giant's Causeway. Some folks say that the rabbits would never have finished their task by nightfall had not the kindly giant Finn Mac Cumhaill come to lend them his aid. Certainly they named the place after him; but, whether or no you give credit to Finn for the carrying, the Rabbit insists that the arrangement and the pattern were his idea.

Next day when the animals awoke the sun was shining. By midday it was blazing in the heavens, and all Ireland began to steam under the unaccustomed heat. Excitedly the animals raked out their bedding to dry in the sun, and, apart from one little bunny who got sunstroke and was sick, everybody was very happy indeed. The second day was just as warm and fine, and so were the days that followed, right through the week.

Then the Horse said, "Doesn't it seem peculiar without any rain? I wouldn't mind a little now and then. Helps to keep the grass sweet."

"That's right," agreed the Cow. "This meadow grass is getting quite parched and dry. Another few days like this and it simply won't be worth eating."

And the Sheep said, "Oh, dear, I'm so hot! I can scarcely drag myself around with all this fleece on me. How shall I bear it?"

"Are you sure you didn't take us too far, Rabbit?" rumbled the Bull. "The animals didn't want to go to the tropics, you know."

"You're nowhere near the tropics," said the Rabbit crossly. "What ungrateful animals you are! I go to all that trouble to bring you into a warm, pleasant climate, and what do you do in return? Grumble—grumble and complain!"

"One extreme's as bad as another," murmured the Horse, as he turned away.

"Don't heed them, Rabbit," said the Cat, stretching herself luxuriously in the heat. "This is gorgeous, so it is! I wouldn't change it for anything."

The Rabbit snorted, for he had no desire to gratify the Cat.

By and by all the other animals began to find disadvantages in their new way of life: not only was the grass dried up like hay, but the rivers and ponds were rapidly shrinking, so that both fishes and frogs became alarmed. The frogs, who are noted for plain speaking, voiced loud, raucous complaints to the Rabbit.

"Why didn't you warn us we'd have to make do with a few driblets of water after we came to Spain?" they shouted. "What's going to happen to our little tadpoles if the pond dries up altogether? Never gave them a thought, did you?"

"That's right—blame me!" the Rabbit retorted. "I suppose you've never had a dry summer before?"

"Listen," said the eldest Frog, with heavy patience. "When there's going to be a dry summer we frogs know about it beforehand and make our preparations by placing the frog-spawn out in the middle of the pond, so that the tadpoles, when they hatch, will have plenty of water to swim about in—but when some interfering busybody like yourself comes along and, without warning, shifts the whole country into another climate, then we don't know where we are. No good result can be expected from interference with the course of nature."

"That's right," said the fish, in their swishy voices. "We agree."

"Let's go back," rumbled the Bull.

"Oh, yes!" cried the Horse and Sheep and Cow. "Let's go back where we were!"

"No! No! No!" shouted the Rabbit obstinately. "Here we are and here we stay!" And, deaf to their pleadings, he went down into the depths of his burrow and stayed there. He wouldn't come out to speak to anybody. Meanwhile the animals above ground sweltered and groaned under the burning sun.

Then one day the Rabbit had a visitor. It was Lochag Mouse. He tiptoed in very timidly, and—"Rabbit!" he whispered.

"What do you want?" said the Rabbit.

Lochag came closer. "Do you know what that is?" he said, laying a shrivelled leaf in the Rabbit's paw.

The Rabbit regarded it silently. "No," he answered at last, "I don't recognize it. What is it?"

"It's the shamrock. All over Ireland the shamrock is shrivelling up and dying. There soon won't be a blade left. I didn't want to bother you, Rabbit, but I thought you ought to know."

"The shamrock?" exclaimed the Rabbit, jumping to his feet. "The emblem of our country withering away? That's terrible. Ireland wouldn't be Ireland without the shamrock. Show me, Lochag."

Together they went up to the entrance of the Rabbit's burrow. The Rabbit flinched as the intense glare of light met his eyes.

"Anywhere you look you'll notice it," said Lochag, plucking a leaf at random and pattering back to the Rabbit's side with it. "See!"

The Rabbit contemplated the shrunken, dried-up leaf, and his heart misgave him. Swallowing hard, he said, "Oh, Lochag, what shall we do?" (It was the only time in his life the Rabbit ever asked anybody's advice, the time he said to Lochag Mouse, "What shall we do?")

"You won't be cross with me if I say?" whispered Lochag.

"Of course not. Sure, I'm never cross with you," the Rabbit replied.

"Very well, then," said Lochag. "If you take my advice, Rabbit, you'll go back."

The Rabbit shook his head hopelessly. "The animals would never consent to do all that pushing again."

"Wouldn't they just?" cried Lochag. "You try them! They're all longing to go back—all but the Cat."

Sure enough, Lochag was right, for the very moment the word went round that the Rabbit was taking them back the delighted animals trooped off and lined themselves in readiness along the south coast. "We're going home again!" cried the excited little bunnies, embracing one another. "Home to the sweet, soft rain!" said the Sheep sentimentally. "Home to the long, lush grass!" sighed the Cow. Only one animal was not pleased: refusing her help, the Cat ran and concealed herself in one of the limestone caverns on the Cuilcagh Mountain, and the place where she hid is called the Cat's Hole to this day.

"I understand now," remarked the Bull, as he laid his shoulder to the rock, "why my Spanish cousins fight so much. It's because they're too hot. They ought to come north with us and cool off a bit!"

In less time than they had thought possible the animals had pushed Ireland back to where it had been in the beginning. As if with relief, the land settled back on its old foundations. Almost at once a fresh breeze blew from the west, bringing a drift of rain, and the parched land opened its thirsty mouth to soak in the moisture.

At the entrance to the Rabbit's burrow Lochag Mouse sat and regarded the scene with satisfaction. "The shamrock's coming on nicely," he reported to the Rabbit, who was busy inside. "Ireland will soon be herself again, nice and soft and damp and homely."

Near by a silly little Mouse—Lochag's nephew, as a matter of fact—began to sing. "Rain, rain, go to Spain——" he chanted.

The Rabbit came out of his hole like a thunderbolt. "If I ever catch you at that again——" he shouted. But the Rabbit's threat went unfinished, for the little Mouse was already over the hills and far away, running for his life. He didn't stop, either, till he got to the far side of the Sperrin Mountains.

2

The Sheep's Gift

_{~~~~~~~~~~~~~~~~~~~~~~~~~~~~~~~~}

In the days when St Columcille was living in Ireland, before he went to Iona, it happened that he was gathering money and gifts to establish a great monastery in Ulster, so that the people might have Christian teaching. Now, St Columcille was the friend of all animals, and they loved him; therefore, when they saw that the King himself had laid his gift of gold before the altar and that other people had followed suit, down to the humblest peasant with his few pence, they felt that they too would like to offer their help. A little deputation was formed, consisting of the Horse, Cow, Dog, and Rabbit, and together they made their way through the oak-woods of Derry to the humble cell that was the home of the saint. As they journeyed they talked of the proposed new monastery and the difference it would make to them.

"We shall be better off than ever before," said the Horse, "for when the Irish folk are all Christians like St Columcille they will treat us kindly and not expect of us more than any animal can do."

"Sure, we're always well treated," said the Dog.

"You may be," put in the Rabbit, "but every animal couldn't say the same."

"One thing I like about the saints," observed the Horse, "is that they realize just how important we are. After all, it was an animal who showed St Patrick where to build his church."

B

"That's right," agreed the Dog. "He built it where the white deer and her fawn rested."

All this time the Cow, pursuing a line of thought of her own, had not spoken. Then suddenly she said, "Do you know what I was thinking? We should have asked the Sheep to come along with us. She's such a good animal that nothing would please her more than to help build a church or monastery."

"We should indeed," said the Horse. "She could make a good contribution, too, with all that wool to dispose of," he added reflectively. "How about sending Dog or Rabbit back to fetch her?"

"Oh, *no!*" said the Rabbit crossly. "It would take all day to explain anything to the Sheep. I couldn't have the patience to wait for her."

"Yes, let's go on," urged the Dog. "She'll bring her gift all right, you'll see. Hasn't she been devoted to the saints ever since she met St Patrick on the side of Slemish Mountain when he was a shepherd boy there? She was the first friend he had."

"All the more reason for asking her," the Cow maintained. "I'll go back."

"It's too late now, Maida," said the Horse. "We're nearly there."

When they reached the door of the cell the Dog barked, and straightway St Columcille appeared, a dove resting on his shoulder, and came forward to greet them.

Then they all sat down on the grass in front of his door, and the animals told the saint of their desire to help him in the building of his monastery.

"I am very strong," explained the Horse, "and I can bring the building-stones to any place where you would wish to have them."

"And once the monastery is built I'll guard it for you with my life," promised the Dog.

"When the monks come to live in it I'll supply them with milk and butter and cheese," offered the Cow.

There was a pause, and then the Rabbit spoke. "I've never thought of it before," he admitted, "but I suppose I'm not really a very useful animal to mankind. I'm not strong, and I haven't got anything to fight with, and the only commodity I can offer you is some rabbit-wool to line the monks' cowls, if they'd like that. I can run very fast, though—would that be any good? Could you employ me as your messenger, do you think?"

"I'm his messenger," interrupted the dove perched on St Columcille's shoulder.

St Columcille put up his hand and stroked her feathers. "I have plenty of work for you both," he said, "for all of you, indeed. Every creature has his own particular talents, and it is a joy to me to see the animal kingdom so ready to lay them at the feet of God. Rabbit, do not despair because you are small and defenceless. In my Good Book I read that the meek shall inherit the earth."

"That's him all right," chuckled the Dog, "with his large family!"

The Rabbit looked so offended that St Columcille hastily intervened, and proceeded to name a day when all the animals who wished could come to him at Derry with their gifts for the new monastery. The Rabbit was allotted the task of informing those in the immediate neighbourhood, while the dove was sent out to tell the animals who lived away at the farther end of Ireland.

By sunrise on the day St Columcille had chosen every road into Derry was thronged with animals. On hoofs and paws and trotters and pads and wings they surged forward, all making for the clearing in the oak-wood. Their excitement mounted as, one by one, they left the great gathering and went up to St Columcille, who wrote down in a golden book their names and the nature of the gift each had promised.

As day wore on, and the animals came and went, St Columcille realized that of all those he had expected only the Sheep had not yet appeared. A shadow crossed his face as he thought of her; he had been depending on her to provide the wool for the robes of his monks, but the Sheep was the special friend of St Patrick and might not care to bring her gifts to another. Columcille sighed, then turned with a welcoming smile to greet the humble little Donkey who had come all the way from County Galway and was standing before him with hanging head, waiting to be noticed.

The Cow too was worried by the Sheep's absence. She still had a notion at the back of her mind that the Sheep had been slighted and her feelings hurt, so, slipping out of the chattering, noisy throng of animals (most of whom had not seen one another for years and years), the Cow wended her way up into the hills, calling as she went. At last there came an answering bleat, and she discovered the Sheep lying in the shelter of a dry ditch.

"Maida!" cried the Sheep. "Oh, Maida, I am glad to see you! There hasn't been a soul about all day, and I badly wanted some one to take a message for me to St Columcille. Would you go back, like a good creature, and tell him that he can have my fleece to make warm clothing for his monks? Will you do that?"

"I will, surely," responded the Cow, "but Agnes, my dear, what's to hinder you from coming yourself? You know, I was quite anxious about you. Are you all right?"

"Just resting," said the Sheep. "I'll perhaps get along later, but, in case I don't arrive in time, you'll deliver my message without fail, won't you?"

"I'll go straight away," promised the Cow, "but whatever will St Columcille think?"

The Sheep smiled mysteriously. "He'll understand by and by," was all she would say.

The animals had quietened down and were sitting in a ring in the clearing of the oak-woods when the Cow returned. St Columcille had thanked them all, and before they departed was giving them the blessing of God on their return journey. He was just about to close the great golden book when he heard the Cow lowing from the edge of the clearing, "Bó! Bó!"

"Yes, Maida?" he said gently, when she came panting up to him. Then the Cow gave him the Sheep's message, and St Columcille inscribed Agnes's name the last in the book. As he did so the Cow heard him murmur to himself, "Food, clothing, and a roof over our heads. . . . Thank God! Thank God!"

Most of the animals were going now, as darkness was beginning to fall, but when St Columcille saw that the Cow was tired with her double journey he invited her to stay in the oak-woods till the morning. The Horse and Dog and Rabbit decided to stay with her, and the Goat and Donkey asked if they might be included too, since they each had such a long journey in front of them—the one to County Kerry and the other to Connemara. St Columcille willingly consented, and the six animals prepared for sleep. The Horse and the Donkey nodded, standing on their feet; the Dog turned three times in a circle and curled up into a ball, his nose under his paw; and the Rabbit, for warmth and company, snuggled in beside the Cow. At first the Goat was restless and fidgety, then he too settled down to sleep. For a while the Cow lay tranquilly munching, only flicking her ears occasionally in the night airs and listening to the little noises that came from the woods; then gradually she dozed off, and nothing more could be heard but the gentle breathing of the animals at peace.

They were awakened at dawn by sounds of activity coming from the saint's cell. Columcille, his morning devotions already performed, was drawing water from the spring, while the dove fluttered over him, lighting now here, now there, and talking to him all the time in her bubbling, croodly voice.

"These saints!" exclaimed the Goat irritably. "They get up in the middle of the night!"

The Dog yawned, stretched himself, and went off to the well for a drink; and the Rabbit sat up and began to do his toilet. He was in the middle of brushing his whiskers when he stopped, listened intently, and then prodded the Cow with his hind foot. "Maida!" he said in her ear. "Do you hear anything?"

From away in the distance there came a faint bleating.

The Cow struggled to her feet. "It's Agnes," she said. She hastened across the clearing to meet her friend, while the Rabbit ran off to St Columcille with the good news that the Sheep had arrived at last.

The other animals were gathered round St Columcille, watching, when the Cow reappeared, followed by the Sheep. They came very slowly, and in a moment everybody saw why, for at Agnes's heels trotted a little new-born lamb. He was so small and young that he staggered as he walked and sometimes sat down quite unexpectedly, but at last he and his mother reached St Columcille's feet.

"Blessed Columcille," said the Sheep, bowing her

head, "I have brought my gift to God, to His Holy Church, and to you. The fleece was not enough—that costs me nothing. The lamb is my gift."

"The lamb is my gift"

St Columcille bent and took up the little lamb in his arms.

"What can I say, Agnes?" he murmured softly. "I am ashamed of myself. When you did not come yesterday I misjudged you, yet you have proved yourself the most faithful of all the animals. Though your name was written last in the book you need not grieve, for did not our Master say that in His Kingdom the last shall be first? Keep your little son, Agnes, until he is fully grown, and then you can bring him back to us and the monks will receive him with joy." So saying, he kissed the lamb on the top of his curly head, restored him to his mother, and made the sign of blessing over them both.

But the jealous Goat said, "Humph! She's getting a special blessing, sending her son into the Church!"

St Columcille regarded him sadly. "Puck," he said, "will you never learn? Good as you animals all are, it is Agnes who has taught us the true meaning of sacrifice; and Agnes's gift is a particularly fitting one, for of all the creatures in the world there was only one to whom our Lord chose to compare Himself—the lamb."

Before he let them go St Columcille told them once more the story they never tired of hearing: how, long ago, the song of the angels came to the sheep lying in the hills above Bethlehem; how the little ass faithfully carried Mary, the Mother of Jesus, to the place appointed; how, when all men closed their doors against the Holy Family, it was the animals who took them into shelter, and the cow who gave up her manger to be a cradle for the Christ Child.

"I love to hear that story," sighed the Horse. "It makes me feel proud to be an animal!"

"It's true, you know," said the Dog thoughtfully. "Though man fails, the animals are still faithful."

They said their good-byes then, and St Columcille accompanied them to the edge of the clearing. Only the Rabbit hesitated as the others began to move away.

"Whisper!" he said, and beckoned with his paw.

St Columcille bent low to hear what the Rabbit had to say.

"Don't you think—" the little animal began hesitantly "—I know you didn't mention it—but don't you think there might have been a rabbit there that night? In the stable, I mean, when the Holy Baby was born?

St Columcille bent low to hear what the Rabbit had to say

You see, there's a tradition in our family that Jesus, as a little boy, played with a rabbit, and loved it because it was soft and cuddly and wouldn't do Him any harm. . . . So I wondered if, maybe, on that night there could have been a rabbit watching—hidden away in the straw, perhaps—a little rabbit that nobody noticed?"

His eyes were full of pleading as he spoke. St Columcille smiled kindly. "I'm *sure* there was!" he said, and the Rabbit kicked up his heels for joy and ran off into the sunshine.

3

The Coming of the Bees

~~~~~~

It was Brother Conan who looked after the bees. He had done so ever since he came to the monastery as a young novice and, wandering into the garden on his second day, lonely and a little afraid, found kind old Brother Anselm pottering among his hives.

"How like it is to my father's garden at home!" sighed Conan, a wave of homesickness making his voice falter.

"Sure, it's part of the same thing," remarked Brother Anselm, glancing up from his work. "Isn't the whole world the garden of our Father in heaven? Come here, brother, till I show you the wisest and most wonderful of all His creatures."

Conan drew near to watch and listen.

"The ancients made a close study of the bees," Brother Anselm went on. "Indeed, I have read in Pliny of a Roman aristocrat who had a transparent hive constructed, so that he could observe the doings of its inhabitants. Not that I'd go so far as that—the beasts have their right to privacy the same as ourselves. Look at that, now!"

Conan felt his arm clutched, and involuntarily his gaze followed Anselm's. "Do you mark yon thieving wasp?" whispered the older man. "He thinks to raid the honey store while nobody's looking. Poor foolish fellow, let him wait till the sentries at the gate catch him!"

The yellow and black body of the wasp quivered intensely in the sunshine before the door of the hive; then he slipped in unobtrusively after a worker bee. Presently Conan saw two bees struggle out to the light, dragging a burden as big as themselves—the dead body of the marauding wasp. Together they flew off with the corpse, dropped it on the far side of the garden wall, and returned to the hive.

"They give a fellow-bee decent burial," remarked Brother Anselm, with a wry smile. "I've watched them cover the body with earth and leaves. But they sing no anthems over a covetous wasp."

"My father had ever a great word of the bees," said Conan suddenly. "He told me that when his grandmother was dying he saw the soul fly from her mouth in the shape of a bee."

Brother Anselm glanced round before replying. "It were well not to mention such things before the Abbot," he murmured. "He would call them foolish fancies—or worse."

"I shall remember," said Conan.

"Indeed," said Brother Anselm, "if we could but realize it the bees offer instruction for each one of us—they who are the perfect community, loyal, industrious, resourceful, and God-fearing. Yes, God-fearing too," he repeated, seeing a look of faint surprise cross Conan's face. "Don't disturb them if they crawl over your feet and habit, brother, they're only getting to know you. Now, what was I saying? Ah, yes, let me tell you a story. The Abbot would call it mere legend—but who knows?"

So the old man and the novice sat on a bench, with their backs propped against the sun-warmed monastery wall, while Brother Anselm talked in a slow, melodious voice not unlike the humming of his charges.

"Once upon a time there was a bee-keeper," he began, "and he was a very greedy man. No matter how much honey his bees produced, it wasn't enough, and one season, when disease spread among them and two or three swarms died, he was like to go out of his mind over the loss. And then he thought of a way to prosper his bees. Next morning he rose early and went to Mass, but the moment the priest had placed the consecrated wafer on his tongue the unrighteous man slipped out of the church and sped homeward. Once there, he pushed the holy wafer into the first hive. Whatever happens to the other three, he said to himself, my first hive is sure to be blessed and yield much honey. Time wore on—as time does with all of us, brother—and in the autumn the greedy man opened his beehives. In three of them there was no honey; but in the fourth the bees had built a little chapel of honeycomb, a waxen shrine complete with roof and columns and pinnacles and altar, and on the altar, amid praises and music, they had laid the consecrated host. When the people of the district saw it they marvelled greatly at the piety and industry of the bees; they banished the avaricious man from their midst, but the bees they cherished, calling them the handmaids of God."

There was silence for a few moments, then said Conan, "I should count myself happy if I could help you to look after them."

"With the Abbot's permission you shall," Brother Anselm replied. "I have need of a helper such as you— some one who does not excite my poor bees, but who will care for them and esteem them. See how they have taken to you already, wise creatures that they are!"

That was how Conan became assistant bee-keeper to the monastery, a task he fulfilled with cheerfulness and devotion; and in the course of time, when good old Brother Anselm died, Conan did not forget that his first duty was to tell the bees. He went out into the garden, and, stopping before each of the hives in turn, he tapped gently with his knuckle and whispered, "Bees, my brethren, your good master Anselm is dead, God rest his soul. It is I, Conan, who will tend you now. Are you willing to stay with me?" Then, as he listened, from inside each hive came a low, deep humming, and Conan was satisfied, knowing that the bees would remain.

Brother Anselm had been mad enough, but never— no, never—the monks declared, was there anyone so crazy as Conan about his bees. Why, he treated them like Christian souls, and spoke of them as though they held the wisdom of the ages! And when the Abbot chose a little party of monks, Conan among them, to establish a new religious foundation in the South of Ire- land the only favour Conan requested was that he should be allowed to take with him three hives of his bees. "They are wiser than we," he said, "and will surely guide us to the right place; and as we travel their humming will be music in our ears."

For many days the little band of exploring monks sailed in their ship, until at length they came to a level, sandy shore backed by dunes and flat fields.

"What if we should stay here?" suggested the first monk, who had grown weary of the motion of the boat and longed to be at peace.

"There is no shelter here," objected the second man, "not even a tree."

"Let us ask Conan," laughed the third. "Tell him to consult his oracles, the bees!"

Somewhat unwillingly Conan opened one of the hives. At once a party of bees flew out, foolhardily, as it happened, for a sudden sharp gust of wind took and dispersed them, driving them into the sand. Only one, who had landed in the bottom of the boat, managed to crawl back into the hive unassisted, and Conan had much ado to recover the rest.

"The answer of the bees," said Conan, when he had gathered them all in again, "is that here the east wind is chilly and harsh, and the sand is blown far inland, smothering the green pastures."

"They are right," agreed the second monk. "Let us seek farther."

The next time the monks landed it was at a river-mouth. They were so glad to step ashore that they scarcely noticed how the ground yielded under their feet and each imprint sucked in a film of muddy water. It was the bees who cried out in panic-stricken protest when Conan laid their hive upon the ground and they felt it settle into the ooze.

"There is no firm foundation here," said Conan indignantly, and, plucking up the hives, he strode back to
the boat.

By and by the ship containing the monks and the beehives turned into Waterford harbour, and by nightfall
they had drawn up along the quays, under the bastion
tower of Reginald the Dane. From a cluster of mud huts
which lined the shore groups of fisherfolk came to stare
in silence at the strange craft with its crew of men in
outlandish robes and sandals, men who carried with
them no treasure that anyone could see save their parch-
ments and drinking vessels and three mysterious wicker
caskets in the stern.

"We could do worse than remain here," said the
eldest monk.

"Indeed, it would be fine to be near the sea-coast,"
remarked another, hankering after the security he had
left behind.

"Methinks the people are not unfriendly," said a
third.

"Nor friendly either," retorted the fourth. "My
brethren, to stay here hugging the quayside will not
earn us a living. We must strike inland. We need lands
to till, and room to plant orchards——"

"And flowers for the bees," said Conan.

Next day at dawn the monks began to move inland,
up the river Suir. The sails were folded now, and they
took it in turn to row, passing oak-woods and castles
and fortresses on their cliffs and a great rock that sat
astride the river-bed. Then the valley opened out before
them, and they could see lush pastures and fields stretching in coloured ribbons away to the foot of a fair
mountain, and the breeze came laden with the scent of
meadow-sweet.

"Let us moor the boat here," said the eldest monk, "for this must surely be the place to which God was conducting us."

Eagerly the others clambered on to the river-bank and hastened after their leader—all except Conan, whose turn it was to guard the boat. Their voices carried to him in the clear air.

"Here are oak-trees in plenty for the building of our monastery," cried one, slapping the trunk of the tree to test its firmness.

"This piece of rising ground would make an ideal site for it," said another.

"The soil is the best I have ever seen," declared the third, stooping to rub the granules of earth between his fingers and sniff its rich aroma.

"The fresh water would be very near," added a fourth.

And it is more beautiful than anything I had imagined! whispered Conan to himself. Nobody heard him: only the water gave a little flurry of excitement and a willow-tree bowed low to the stream in acknowledgment of his tribute. All at once he was aware that a little girl had stolen up along the river-bank and was eyeing him covertly from the shadow of the willow-tree.

"Tell me, little one," said the monk, "what is the name of your attractive mountain yonder?"

"Slievenamon," answered the girl, "which is to say, 'the mountain of fair women.'" And she smiled that a monk should ask that name.

"And the pleasant valley that lies before us—what is it called?" he asked her.

"It is called Clonmel," she replied, "that is, 'the honey meadow.'"

"Praise be to God!" cried Conan. "The answer to

our prayers!" And without hesitation he opened the doors of his three beehives and released the long-imprisoned bees. But before they left him the bees did an extraordinary thing. From the hive in the centre they streamed out and up, till the throng stood erect in a column over his head; then from the right and the left more bees came in, until as Conan watched he saw them form a living cross hung against the sky. Only for a moment did they hover there, then at his whispered "Godspeed!" the cross dissolved into air as the bees winged their way with joyful buzzing to savour the clover and the meadow-sweet and the gorse on the hillside.

So intent were the other monks on examining the soil and measuring the land and testing the timber that not one of them saw the sign of blessing in the heavens, the sign that the bees had made. Nobody saw it but Conan. And wasn't that only right? For, after all, it was Conan who loved the bees!

C

4

How the Donkey found his Fortune

~~~~~~~~~~~~~~~~~~~~~~~~~~~~~~~~~~~

I

It was a bright June day, and the Hare on the Bluestack Mountains grew restless.

"Let's go and seek our fortune," he said, bounding over to the Donkey.

"Donkeys have no fortune," said the little Ass resignedly.

"Nonsense! You have your good days and your bad days like the rest of us," replied the Hare.

"My bad days and my worse days," said the Donkey. "Days when my turf-creels are full to the top, and days when Seanín gets on my back as well, till I stumble on the stones and my legs be nearly breaking under me."

"I wouldn't stand it," the Hare affirmed. "Indeed I wouldn't. You've been working for nothing far too long. Why don't you take the law into your own hooves and run away?"

"Too tired," sighed the Donkey. "Sure, the spirit's all druv out of me with the overwork!"

"I've plenty of spirit for the two of us," said the Hare. "Come on, Paudeen, cheer up! You'll never be a day younger, so you might as well come with me now and see a bit of the world."

The Donkey stood for a long time reflecting. Then he said, "I suppose I might as well. I can't be much worse off than I am here—though it could be that I'm daft entirely to be trusting myself to a mad March Hare!"

"Enough of that!" put in the Hare. "I'm not mad at this time of year—only merry."

So Paudeen the Donkey and Flick the Hare set off to seek their fortune. The Donkey stepped on his neat little hoofs along the grassy margin of the road, and the Hare ran in the fields by his side and chatted to him through the hedge. Now and then they stopped for something to eat—a few mouthfuls of juicy grass or a carrot or a turnip. They liked much the same things to eat, and that is a great aid to friendship.

In this way the Hare and the Donkey came down through the Barnesmore Gap and reached the shores of Lough Eask, where they decided to spend the night.

Flick was up early in the morning, paddling along the edge of the lake looking for pearls, but he didn't find any; and soon the two friends were on their way again, shaping their course for the town of Donegal. Lots of other animals seemed to be going there too, and at last the Hare, in an urgent whisper, summoned the Donkey into the field beside him.

"Listen, Paudeen," he said, "there must be a fair in the town, and it wouldn't be safe for us to go through when it's so crowded. If I as much as showed my nose there every dog in the place would be after me; and you'd run the risk of getting caught, too. We'd better bypass the town altogether."

"Ach, no," pleaded the Donkey. "I've never been in Donegal town before, and maybe I'll never have the chance again. I'd like fine to have a look at the fair, so I would."

"You're taking a risk on yourself," warned the Hare.

"When people see a donkey on the loose they know he's run away from his master and they try to capture him. I'm telling you, mind!"

But the Donkey stuck out his lower lip in the obstinate way that donkeys have, and Flick knew it was no use arguing with him. The two friends agreed to meet again at the first crossroads beyond the town on the way to the west. So they parted, and the Donkey trotted by himself between the rows of houses and into the market square. It was thronged with people and animals, as the Hare had said, and the noise they all made filled the Donkey with excitement. First he passed a group of cows lined up along the pavement; then he saw sheep in a pen, with a collie dog set to watch them; he passed hens in coops, and goats with their legs spancelled, and little pigs huddled together in the well of a cart—and the Donkey felt so pleased with himself, walking about wherever he wanted to go, just like a human being, that his heart sang for joy. Oh, it's a grand fair, he said to himself. I wouldn't have missed it for worlds!

Before a stall where a woman sold vegetables the Donkey hesitated. There were some tempting carrots lying just within his reach, and the woman was talking so hard he was sure she would never notice him. Without thinking twice, Paudeen pulled a carrot off the stall, and was beginning to crunch it in his teeth when all of a sudden the woman fetched him a blow on the rump and cried, "Who's in charge of this ass? Who owns the thieving donkey, eh?"

She was coming at him again with arm raised, and Paudeen, in his efforts to escape her, backed into an array of aluminium saucepans spread on the ground before a neighbouring stall. All was clatter and confusion then; every way the Donkey turned he seemed to do more damage, until at last he found himself encircled by an angry crowd.

"Who owns the ass?" every one was asking every one else. "Who owns the ass?" They appeared never to have heard of an ass who owned himself and was responsible to nobody. A rough man seized Paudeen and, slinging a rope round his neck, dragged him over to the side of the square and tied him to the church railings.

"There!" he said, with an oath. "That'll keep you out of mischief till we see what's to be done with you."

The cows on the pavement looked sympathetically at Paudeen, but they could do nothing for him; and the poor little captive Donkey hung his head in misery, wondering what would become of him now.

Meanwhile the Hare squatted behind the hedge out by the crossroads and waited for his friend. He nibbled the grass, and he blew dandelion clocks to know what time it was, and he even ran out on to the road to see if the Donkey was coming, but there wasn't sight nor sound of Paudeen. At last the Hare ventured into the town to look for the Donkey. He kept along by the backs of the houses and inquired of a passing Cat coming from the fair, and she directed him to go through the long grass of the churchyard to where Paudeen was, on the other side of the railings.

"Paudeen!" whispered the Hare, when he had got near enough. "Don't look round, Paudeen. It's me— Flick. Are you tied?"

The Donkey nodded gloomily.

"I'll try and bite the rope through," said the Hare. "Stand still, so that they won't see me. The minute I give the word run for your life!"

The ground in the churchyard was higher than the pavement, and the Hare was at just the right level to tackle the rope. With great determination he bit and chewed and pulled and snapped, till at last the rope fell apart.

"Run!" urged Flick, and the Donkey set off as fast as he could gallop down the street. Once a man ran out to intercept him, but like lightning Flick jumped through the railings and flashed between the man's legs so that he tripped and fell headlong in the roadway.

On and on the two friends ran, until they were sure they had left the town of Donegal far behind; then, panting with exertion, they turned into a field and collapsed on the grass. There they lay all afternoon, resting in the cool of the trees and listening to the song of the lark in the bright sky.

"That was a near thing!" sighed the Donkey at last. "If it wasn't for you, Flick——"

"Say no more!" the Hare requested, with a modest wave of the paw. "Say no more! You'll know better the next time, Paudeen."

"Indeed I will," said the Donkey. "I was foolish to go into the town at all, but when I pinched that carrot I must have been a silly Ass!"

The Hare chuckled. "If I had done it they'd have called me hare-brained," he said. "But take my advice, Paudeen—never trust a human being, or go near one at all if you can help it."

"It's a terrible thing, surely, if none of them is to be trusted," said the Donkey.

"That's my experience, anyway," answered the Hare. "I've learned to keep a safe distance from them."

"Oh, dear, oh, dear," sighed the Donkey, "and here was I, hoping to find a good master at the end of my travels!"

"Well, if that's what you call a fortune you're welcome to it," said the Hare. "But you've a lot of the world to see yet, Paudeen. How about putting another couple of miles past us before nightfall?"

"Oh, I couldn't!" the Donkey protested. "I'm far too weary."

But the Hare by this time had quite recovered his lively spirits and could not sit still.

"What do you say to having a little dance to celebrate your freedom?" he suggested.

"Dear, but you have the itchy paws!" exclaimed the Donkey. "I tell you, Flick, I couldn't stir a hoof to-night; but you dance and I'll clap."

"All right," said the Hare. "I'll wait for the moon coming up. I always dance better in the moonlight."

So as soon as the moon had climbed high enough to light a stage for him among the trees the Hare began to dance. Up and down the turf he frolicked, bounding and leaping and singing as he went. This is the song of Flick the Hare:

> I'm a merry March Hare,
>   A mad Hare am I!
> It's myself does make the crazy leaps,
>   Reaching for the sky.
>
> I kick and I skip
>   And I birl right round—
> Three paws of me are in the air
>   And one on the ground.
>
> I can turn a somersault,
>   I can beat a tune;
> So come, come and dance with me
>   Underneath the moon. . . .
>
> Come, Paudeen, and dance with me
>   To my merry tune!

Fascinated, the Donkey lay and watched the antics of the Hare. Now and again, as he flashed by, Flick would call on Paudeen to come and join the dance, but the Donkey shook his head and contented himself with applauding.

I'll dance, he said to himself, the day I find a good master; not till then.

He spun round and round on one toe

"Watch me do *Swan Lake*!" cried Flick, and he glided out of the bushes, pirouetting on his two back paws and weaving his front paws gracefully in the air. On reaching the centre of his moonlit stage he spun round and round on one toe so fast that the Donkey's eyes were dazzled.

"You're making me dizzy!" called Paudeen, and the Hare dropped his ballet pose and came down on all fours again.

"Want a change?" he shouted. "All right, this is me jitterbugging! Hotcha!"

The Hare's feet moved like lightning as he kicked and stamped on the ground, and the grass began to fly out round him as if from a mowing-machine.

Just then an owl hooted indignantly in the branches overhead. The owl was in charge of the clearing, and was not going to have it spoiled by any mere animals of passage. "Who-o-o are you-ou-ou?" he called, in hollow tones. "Who-o-o? Who-o-o?"

The Donkey shivered down his spine. "Easy on, Flick," he advised his friend. "You'd better stop now; they don't like it. Anyhow, if you don't have a rest you won't be fresh for to-morrow."

"Won't I?" cried Flick, bounding over to where the Donkey lay. "I'll be up first in the morning—wait till you see!"

II

Sure enough, when the Donkey opened his sleepy eyes the following morning the Hare was already up and stirring; in fact, Paudeen surprised Flick in the act of raising a large stone with his paw to peer in below it.

"What are you doing, Flick?" asked the Donkey, full of curiosity.

"Oh, I always do this before I make a journey," said the Hare. "If there are plenty of creepy-crawly things beneath that's lucky; but if there's no life under the stone that would be a bad sign, and wherever I was going I wouldn't go."

"Well, well!" exclaimed the Donkey. "We learn something new every day. But wait a minute, Flick! Let me see the wriggly things, too."

"Hurry up, then," cried the Hare. "This stone is heavy."

But before the slow-moving Donkey could scramble to his feet and get there all the creepy-crawlies had vanished into the ground, and he saw nothing.

"That means good luck for you and none for me," concluded Paudeen gloomily.

"Ach, away out of that, you old pessimist!" cried Flick, dropping the stone into place and giving his friend a playful push. "Aren't we together? Look, we'll lift two more stones and take the best of three." But, however Flick might try to cheer him, the Donkey still started the day feeling a little dispirited—though, as it happened, it was the Hare who had the first stroke of ill-luck.

The countryside lay very calm and quiet before them as they travelled; only the sky was in motion, with big curly clouds bowling in from the Atlantic and at times obscuring the sun.

Flick's nostrils twitched. "I smell rain," he observed. "We'd better get as far as we can by noon." And unconsciously he hurried, so that the Donkey found it difficult to keep pace with him. Paudeen looked longingly at the farmhouses as they passed; and once, when he spied a Dog lying asleep by a doorway, he stopped at the gate and stared in. He looks well fed, he said to himself. I wonder if he has a good master?

"What's keeping you, Paudeen?" called Flick, coming back.

Just then the Dog raised his head and caught sight of the Hare. At once all sleep was forgotten; he dashed out, barking furiously, and began to chase Flick down the road. Flick loped along easily, without bothering to go very fast; for one thing, he did not want to leave the Donkey too far behind, and besides, he enjoyed tantalizing the Dog by keeping just out of his reach. Then something happened to give a jolt to Flick's self-confidence and set the Donkey screaming with fright. Round the bend of the road appeared two young men, and the Hare was running straight towards them! They spread themselves across the road to catch him, the Dog was encouraged to put on an extra spurt, and the Donkey shouted, "Flick, look out! Danger!" But, wheeling to the right, Flick slipped through the wire fence and

The Hare was running straight towards them!

bounded up the hill beyond, knowing well how his powerful hind legs would give him the advantage on the upward slope. A few yards of rough hillside sufficed to stop the Dog; once he had seen the Hare disappear over the crest of the hill he turned back, honour satisfied, and shortly afterwards Paudeen met him on the road making for home, with his two sides heaving like bellows and his pink tongue lolling.

For the first time Paudeen considered his own position. The young men were coming nearer; he could not escape easily through the fence as Flick had done, and it began to look as though the Donkey would be caught instead of the Hare. There was nothing for it but to bend his head and munch the grass at the side of the road, doing his best to look innocent and pretend that he belonged there. Luckily the men gave him only a passing glance.

"I didn't know Dan owned an ass," said one.

"He maybe got it at the fair yesterday," responded the other. "Wouldn't you think he'd be afraid of it wandering?"

"Ach, I don't know," said the first man. "Donkeys seldom go far."

Paudeen longed to tell them what a widely travelled Donkey *he* was; but he judged it more prudent to hold his tongue. As soon as the men had gone he breathed a deep sigh of relief and continued along the road, keeping his eyes open for some lane or pathway that would lead him to the hill where he had last seen the Hare.

By and by, as he approached a dip of riverside meadow, he was surprised to hear some one singing; the strain had such a familiar ring that the Donkey quickened his step and began to canter down the hill. When he came to the bridge at the foot he stopped to look over the parapet—and, right enough, who should be in the field below, dancing among the daisies, but his old friend Flick!

Paudeen had arrived too late for the beginning of the song, but the two verses he did hear went like this:

> The Dog was fat, the Dog was slow—
> You should have heard him puff and blow!
>
> But the Hare was smart and the Hare was slick—
> Sure, there's no Dog born could ever catch Flick!

"You were nearly caught, all the same," said the sober little Donkey, looking down from the bridge.

"Is it yourself, Paudeen?" called the Hare. "I was just putting in the time, waiting for you. Come on down here and dabble your feet in the stream. It's lovely."

Paudeen clambered carefully down by the path which Flick showed him circling the end of the bridge, and soon he too was standing ankle-deep, watching the clear, amber-coloured water swirl away the dust from his hoofs.

"You were nearly caught, all the same"

"Isn't this great!" sighed the Donkey, blissfully closing his eyes.

"It's very pleasant, certainly," the Hare agreed, "though you know, Paudeen, you can't claim to have had a real paddle till you've been in the sea."

"The sea?" echoed the Donkey, blinking. "What's the sea?"

"Do you really not know?" cried the Hare incredulously. "Paudeen, you must be making fun!"

The Donkey solemnly shook his head. "Cross my heart!" he declared. "I know nothing about it, Flick. Sure, what have I ever seen all my life until now except heather and stones and turf—and the mist that does be on the bog?"

"Well, aren't you the ignorant animal!" the Hare teased him. "I'm thinking it's a good thing you came with me to improve your education. We had glimpses of the sea all the way along here, but I never even thought of mentioning it. The sea, I would have you understand, Paudeen, is a vast, wonderful stretch of water going so many measureless miles into the distance that nobody can see to the end of it."

"Is that all?" said the Donkey. He sounded disappointed, for he had no great love of water.

"But it's not ordinary water," Flick went on, anxious to impress his friend. "It doesn't lie flat and still like a pond. No, it hisses and roars, and sometimes it even jumps up and hits you."

"I don't think I'll like it at all, then," said Paudeen. "I've been hit too often already."

"Oh, you'll love it!" cried the Hare confidently. "Everybody loves the sea. Just wait till you see it at Fintragh Bay or below Kilcar, and give me your opinion then!"

"Very well," said Paudeen. "I'll take a little sip of it to please you, anyway."

The Hare laughed. "You don't drink it, you—you—Donkey!" he said. "It's not ordinary water, I tell you, such as an animal can drink. You'll soon realize why.

Sea-water has a most peculiar taste, and it only makes you thirstier."

"How very odd!" commented Paudeen. "What's it for?"

But even the Hare didn't know the answer to that one—not at first, though after a few moments' concentrated thought he announced that the sea must be there for the sake of the fishes, and with that conclusion Paudeen had to be content.

By now the marching battalions of clouds had drawn to a halt and were massing overhead; the colours of the summer landscape sank, dimmed, into a grey wash of light; there was an uneasy expectancy in the air.

"Let's get moving," said the restless Hare. "I suggest that we keep farther back in the hills. It's much too risky down on the road."

Paudeen, still slightly unnerved by their recent encounter with the two men, willingly agreed; but once they had climbed on to the hillside he found the going as rough and stony as anything he had experienced when he was in the Bluestack Mountains. While the Hare skipped nimbly ahead the Donkey struggled after him, his feet slipping on the stones and entangling themselves in the roots of heather. After a couple of hours of this, when his legs were aching, it was small comfort to Paudeen to see how the Hare, running to and fro and round and round, and covering four times the ground he did, was as bright and lively as when they had first set out.

While they travelled on through the darkening afternoon the Hare beguiled the way with songs of his own composition, or sought to revive his friend's flagging spirits by asking him riddles. He would suddenly come bounding up to Paudeen and shout, "What has ears and can't hear?" Then, without giving the Donkey time to think, he would answer it himself. "Why, barley, of course!" In another minute he was at it again. "What has eyes and can't see? Come on, Paudeen, you must know that one! Think! No? A potato, you silly fellow, a potato!" Paudeen sighed as he trudged along. The Hare made a wide circle round the bushes and boulders and came dashing back to him, full-pelt. "What has legs and can't walk?" he cried breathlessly. "Me," said Paudeen, and sat flat down among the heather.

At first the Hare laughed uproariously. "That's not the right answer at all!" he chortled. "The answer is a stool. You know, human beings use them as perches, instead of sitting like sensible animals on the ground. I've often seen a woman carry one out to the byre at milking-time. Haven't you?" *L/S 12037*

No response came from Paudeen, and when the Hare glanced in his direction he saw to his shock that the Donkey wasn't laughing at all. Paudeen still lay as he had fallen, with his heavy head drooping almost to the dust, while two great tears coursed each other down his nose. Immediately Flick sprang to his feet and darted over to his companion.

"Why, Paudeen!" he cried, full of sympathy, putting his paw round the Donkey's neck. "Paudeen, old fellow, what's come over you at all? Are you ill?"

The Donkey shook his head, but the tears flowed faster than ever.

"Look," said the Hare, glancing up at the threatening sky, "the storm is breaking, and we'll be caught in a torrent of rain if we don't hurry. Could you manage as far as yon bridge, Paudeen?"

"I—I'll try," gulped Paudeen; and, leaving their mountainy track, they struck down across the fields to the road again, reaching it where a fussy little river was spanned by a stone bridge. Under the arch they crawled, none too soon, for already raindrops as big as shillings were plopping all around them. The Donkey stretched

"Paudeen, old fellow, what's come over you at all?"

himself gratefully on the sandy margin of the river, resting his head against the green, mossy ramparts of the bridge; while the Hare, in the intervals of playing 'lep' across the boulders, stood to watch the rain. Heavier it grew, until the view was almost obliterated

D

by the downpour; even the fretted river, stung with raindrops, seemed glad to linger for a moment under the bridge.

"Weren't we the lucky ones to get here in time!" exclaimed Flick. "See, Paudeen, where the spiders have come in for shelter—and, I declare, there's a poor worm who's going to be drowned if nobody rescues him!"

He popped out and popped in again with the worm dangling over his paw. Then, pleased with himself, Flick began to hum a tune. Presently he burst into song.

> Let it rain, let it snow, [he sang]
> Flick the Hare knows where to go!
>
> What although the rain be teeming?
> Somewhere else the sun is beaming. . . .

Then all of a sudden he stopped, for he remembered that the Donkey was sad.

"Go on," said Paudeen.

"Ah, it wasn't a very good song, that one," said Flick. "Must have got damp! Suppose you tell me instead what it was that ailed you a while back, the time you cried?" He squatted down beside the Donkey and gazed earnestly into his eyes.

Paudeen looked uncomfortable. "It was nothing much," he murmured. "Only weariness and a touch of homesickness—that's all!"

"Homesickness?" cried the Hare, startled. "Surely to goodness you're not thinking long for that miserable old shack on the Bluestack Mountains that you were so glad to leave?"

"Oh, no, no," replied the Donkey hastily. "That wasn't the kind of homesickness I meant at all. Somewhere in Donegal I feel sure there's a kind master willing to take me in and treat me well, and I must keep on going until I find him; only between him and me the miles stretch out, so long and wearisome, and when I come to the end of a hard day's travel and know that I'm not much nearer my goal than I was at the beginning, I sometimes lose heart."

"But I thought you wanted to see a bit of the world?" exclaimed the Hare. "You've seen nothing yet."

"All I want," said Paudeen simply, "is a good home. You see, Flick, it may be all very well for you to run wild over mountain and bog, and take your living where you find it—that's the nature of a hare—but a donkey isn't made that way, and he can't do it. This kind of life contents you, but I can't help wondering what will become of me when winter descends and I've no shelter and nowhere to go."

"Winter?" shrieked the Hare. "But, my dear Paudeen, we haven't even had midsummer yet! Why think about winter when it's months away? Are you trying to make yourself miserable, keeping winter the whole year round?"

"It's coming, whatever you say," answered Paudeen dolefully, "and I'd like a roof over my head before it does. Besides, I can't keep up with you, Flick; it worries me; I know I'm only holding you back. Wouldn't you be far better to go ahead by yourself and leave me to plod along at my own speed?"

"Ah, don't say that, Paudeen!" Flick pleaded, impulsively putting his paw on the Donkey's hoof. "Sure, I've never complained, have I? A hare doesn't often look for company, but I've enjoyed yours, Paudeen, and I wouldn't dream of leaving you till I see you settled in your new home."

Then Paudeen was silent, ashamed that he had tried to get rid of the only true friend he had ever had. By and by the Hare said, "Do you know, Paudeen, I was just reflecting that the best place to search for a good master would be in Glencolumbkille. The whole valley was blessed by St Columcille when he lived there, so the people are bound to be kindly folks. Would you care to try?"

"I would," replied the Donkey. "Indeed, indeed I would. How do we reach it?"

"Well, let me see," the Hare began, stroking his nose thoughtfully. "I'd recommend going along by the sea coast as far as Slieve League, and then over the top of the mountain. You get a wonderful view from up there (indeed, I've scores of cousins who wouldn't live anywhere else) and——"

"Which is the shortest way?" interrupted the Donkey.

"The shortest way?" The Hare hesitated. "There's a motor road leading inland from Carrick," he admitted. "You wouldn't find it nearly so interesting, but of course it's easier and more direct. Would you rather go that way, Paudeen?"

"Whatever is the quickest," said Paudeen.

There was a barely perceptible pause, then the Hare agreed. "All right, Paudeen. As soon as the weather fairs I'll take you to Glencolumbkille by the nearest road I know."

III

The rain continued for three days after that, but the Donkey didn't mind, since the delay enabled him to gather his strength for the last lap of his journey. Sometimes he wondered why Flick had become unusually quiet; then, quite by accident, he discovered the reason on the very morning they were leaving.

Paudeen had been wakened early by the welcome glitter of sunshine on the water; he lay for a moment watching the moving pattern of light reflected on the under-side of the bridge; then he rolled over to share with the Hare his gladness that they would have a bright day to walk in—but to his surprise Flick was not there! The form where he had lain in the sand was quite cold; he wasn't eating the grass or paddling in the brook; there was no sign of him anywhere. A moment-ary wave of panic leapt in the Donkey's breast when he found himself alone. Without Flick to guide him how would he ever reach Glencolumbkille in safety? But almost at once he realized that Flick was not the kind of animal to leave a friend in the lurch: he must be some-where around.

Paudeen had ventured a few yards out from the bridge when a faint sound above made him look up, to spy Flick erect on the parapet, gazing into the distance. Before the Donkey had time to call out Flick had leapt down on to the road and disappeared from view. When he came into sight again he was running up the hill beyond; on its crest he halted in the same eager attitude, still and tense, as if straining to see something afar off. Curious, Paudeen followed, careful to make no noise. Just as he reached the summit he heard the Hare give vent to the most heartrending sigh imaginable, and the Donkey stood transfixed, not knowing whether to go on or go back. Flick was quite unaware of having been fol-lowed, and presently he began to talk to himself, as solitary people do. Paudeen heard him murmur wist-fully, "What a beautiful day! We mightn't get another one like it all summer—and I did so want to paddle! Oh, dear! Oh, dear!" Then somehow his words drifted into a plaintive little air set in a minor key. As far as Paudeen could make it out, it went something like this (punctuated with sighs):

> Stay blue and sparkling, sea! Shine, shine, O sun!
> For I'll be coming back to you when my task's done.
> My cousins are dancing all over Slieve League—(*sigh*)
> But my pal's a Donkey who drops with fatigue!
> I did want to paddle; I did want to swim:
> But I mustn't think of that till I've found a home for him.
> Guide me, O Columcille, show me the way,
> Send us health and happiness (*deep sigh*) and another sunny day!

Then the Donkey knew that the Hare was breaking his heart because he couldn't get down to the sea he loved so much. That was why he had risen early, to have a long look at the blue, enticing ocean before he must needs turn his back on it and take the short cut to Glencolumbkille. As Paudeen retreated sadly down the hill he felt more ashamed than ever. I've been a very selfish animal, he said to himself. I must make it up to Flick somehow, before it's too late.

When the Hare reappeared under the bridge the Donkey stretched himself and yawned as though he had only just awakened.

"Come along, lazybones!" cried Flick. "The sun was up hours ago. It's time we were on the move."

"Tell me this, Flick," said the Donkey, blinking his eyes sleepily. "When I live in Glencolumbkille, shall I be able to see the sea?"

"Depends whereabouts you are," answered the Hare. "Unless you're very far back in the glen, I'd say you could."

"Because, you know," Paudeen continued, "you've talked such a lot about it that I should hate to settle down for life without ever having seen the sea. Do you think we might possibly travel the long way after all?"

The Hare caught his breath in delight, and his eyes shone with rapture. "Oh, Paudeen!" he cried, throwing his paws round the Donkey's neck. "Paudeen, that will be simply gorgeous! You've no idea how wonderful it is by the sea on a day like this!" Then he hesitated and looked anxious. "But—but you're sure you'll be able to manage the climb over Slieve League?"

"Certain," replied the Donkey. "Haven't I been four days resting?" (He was determined never again to earn the reproach of being "a Donkey who drops with fatigue"!)

By the early afternoon the two friends had reached the sea. Paudeen guessed they must be nearly there when an unexpected blast of wind smote them in the face, making his eyes sting and laying the Hare's fur flat along his back.

"Ah, the sea-breeze, Paudeen!" exclaimed the Hare, snuffing it up gladly. "And look—there's the sea!"

Paudeen edged into a sheltered cranny, from which he could contemplate the wide expanse of shimmering blue that stretched to meet the sky.

"Isn't it beautiful?" breathed the Hare at his side. "Wait till I get down on the flat sand and I'll dance for you, Paudeen. I'll show you how to do it. When you dance on the sand you leave a lovely pattern of paw-marks all over it. Come on. We mustn't stop here."

The Hare bounded on down through the sandhills, taking agile leaps from one side of the path to the other, while the Donkey slipped and slithered after him, his progress accompanied by cascades of rolling pebbles and miniature avalanches of sand. Soon both animals were at the bottom, and Flick tore across the beach, ran through the lacy edge of the waves, and dashed back again to where Paudeen had stopped in the shadow of a rock.

"Kiss my paw!" demanded the Hare, holding out a wet paw. "Go on, Paudeen—savour the salty taste."

The Donkey gingerly put out the tip of his tongue and licked the wet fur.

"Ugh!" he said, wrinkling up his nose and trying to spit out the taste, while the Hare laughed with delight.

"You're getting your education, Paudeen!" he reminded him. "And now, what about that dance? May I have the pleasure?"

"Not yet, Flick," replied the Donkey, lying down. "I promise you, once I've found a good master I'll dance with you to celebrate my fortune—not until then. But you go ahead on your own."

"All right," said Flick, and he sped away, shouting:

> Oh, Paudeen, it's simply grand
> To chase your shadow along the sand. . . .

For a while the Donkey, with an amused smile, watched the frolics of the Hare; later on, encouraged by Flick, he even risked a paddle—but it was obvious that he was not enjoying it much (he said the receding waves made him feel dizzy), and soon, with an air of relief, Paudeen returned to lie in the warm spot behind the rock, where gradually he nodded off to sleep.

He was aroused by the thud of a body striking the sand beside him; it proved to be Flick, who had discovered the new thrill of racing across the grass and taking a flying leap from the edge of the sandhills. Flick was certainly having the time of his life; but when Paudeen observed how far along the sand the shadow of the rock had crept since he had first lain down, and realized that they must have spent more than two hours at the seashore, he began to bestir himself at once.

"Hallo, there!" called Flick, noticing the Donkey's movement. "I spied you, Paudeen, having forty winks on the sly!" He came running over, his eyes shining with pleasure and excitement. "This has been such a wonderful, wonderful day," he cried, "that I've gathered up all my joy and put it into a song to remember. Would you like to hear my song, Paudeen?"

"I've no objections," said the Donkey.

So, to a brisk and lively air, accompanied by the appropriate gestures, the Hare delivered himself of his latest composition, a happy song to celebrate that memorable summer's day. This is how it ran:

> Scurry down the sandhills,
>   Leap through the air—
> Count, when you land,
>   If your paws are all there!
>
> Race along the seashore
>   With a big splash for fun,
> Up and down, and round and round,
>   As fast as you can run.
>
> Scoot among the seaweed,
>   Swish through the foam,
> Round the rocks and back again,
>   And make a dash for home.
>
> Laugh to see the sunshine,
>   Live without a care:
> That's the way to take the world—
>   Says Flick, the merry Hare!

The last words were scarcely out of his mouth when a stone flung from the sandhills above landed beside him, spraying him with sand. It was followed immediately by another, which came so close that the Hare had to dodge.

"Boys!" he shrieked, and dashed away to hide.

The next moment they came tumbling and rollicking down on to the strand, boys on their way from school, noisy, rough, and ready for any mischief. Paudeen recoiled under his rock, trying to make himself invisible—but in vain, for one of the boys spotted him straight away.

"Oh, look—a donkey!" he shouted. "What luck!"

They dragged Paudeen out of his hiding-place then, and set him to canter up and down the beach, giving them rides in turn. Paudeen would not have minded that so much—he was always willing to give a child a ride, if properly asked—but these were big, coarse boys who cared nothing for a donkey's feelings, but drove their heels into his sides and rained blows and buffets upon him to make him go faster. They shouted and quarrelled, too, about whose turn it was next, and whether Peadar had had a longer ride than Conn, until the poor Donkey felt so frightened and bewildered that he could not understand what they wanted him to do next. Then they called him stupid and kicked him. When he was at the very end of his endurance he was saved by the boy named Conn suddenly saying, "I'm for off, fellows. My ma'll skin me alive if I'm not home for my tea."

"Sure enough," agreed one of the others, "the time must be wearin' on. We'd better quit for now. But we'll come back here after, eh?"

"Put the ass somewhere we can find him easy," advised Peadar. "What do you say to walling him up in yon cave till we get back?"

Together they pushed and manœuvred Paudeen into

a cleft in the rocks and proceeded to roll boulders across the front of it to keep him from escaping. That done, they grabbed their schoolbags and raced home, whooping and yelling and shoving one another off the path.

Their shouts had hardly died away when Paudeen heard a scratching sound outside.

"Is that you, Flick?" he said, in a hoarse whisper.

"It is," answered the Hare. "Are you all right? Oh, Paudeen, these stones are so heavy that I can't shift them at all! Keep your heart up, like a brave fellow, till I run and fetch a bigger animal to help me."

He returned after a while with Cissie Cow. She was very dubious about the whole undertaking, especially when she saw the steep path leading from the sandhills down to the beach.

"Expect me to negotiate that?" she demanded, eyeing Flick accusingly. "What do you think I am—an acrobat?" Before Flick could reply she had answered the question herself. "I'm a respectable, middle-aged matron, I'd have you remember, not one of your nifty little bathing belles, to go skipping over the beach!"

"Only this once, Cissie!" pleaded Flick.

"No regard for age and dignity!" Cissie grumbled, peering down the slope. "And how should I ever manage up again? Tell me that."

"Oh, do come on!" Flick besought her, wringing his paws in desperation. "We'll get you up somehow, Cissie, never fear. You see, it's all my fault that my friend's in this terrible fix, and I've simply got to set him free."

"I suppose I may as well speed the business through when I've gone so far," Cissie murmured. "Keep out of the way, Flick—here I come!"

The Hare made a quick side-step, and Cissie lumbered down the path in hasty and ungainly fashion, ending knee-deep in sand.

"I'd be ashamed all my life if any of my friends saw me do that," she remarked. "It was anything but ladylike."

Cissie lumbered down the path in hasty and ungainly fashion

"Never mind," said Flick. "You're doing a good turn, like a perfect lady. This way."

It was not easy to move the heavy boulders that imprisoned the Donkey, but Cissie and Flick worked hard with horns and hoofs and paws until at last they had made an opening large enough for Paudeen to squeeze through.

"Thank you—oh, thank you!" cried Paudeen, scrambling into the open. "Shut up there in the darkness, I began to be so afraid that I'd never, never see Glencolumbkille after all."

"Is it the Glen you're heading for?" inquired Cissie, full of interest. "Then be sure and give my love to the old place, for that's where I was born and reared. And I'll tell you this, now I have the chance: if ever you should happen to want something extra-special ask for it at the stone cross of St Columcille and you'll be sure to get it."

"Honest?" said Paudeen, his eyes wide.

"I've proved it," Cissie answered. "St Columcille always hears an animal's prayer."

"I'll remember," said the Donkey.

Flick ran lightly up the pathway, and unthinkingly Paudeen was beginning to follow when they were arrested by an angry shout from below. "Here, you two!" called Cissie, firmly planted in the sand. "How about me?"

"Oh, dear!" whispered Flick, agitated. "I wish she wouldn't make such a fuss, because we really can't afford to be delayed. Somebody's bound to come along and pull her up."

"We couldn't leave her after all she's done," Paudeen reproved him, and he started back down again for the last time.

Cissie bent her head so that Flick could grasp her horns, and Paudeen stationed himself behind her, ready to push; then, at the signal of "Yo, heave ho!" from Flick, they all began pulling and pushing and struggling, until at last Cissie reached the top with a rush, bowling Flick over in a backward somersault as she came. "Hurrah!" shouted Flick, when he had got himself the right way up again. "You're the Cow who could storm Dublin Castle any day, Cissie!"

"Did ever I think I'd come to this at my time of life!" gasped Cissie. "You certainly never know what you can do till you try. Come with me, the pair of you, and I'll bring you to a safe lodging before I say good-night."

Cissie's choice proved to be a comfortable nook under a haystack, so secluded that the searching boys never came even within half a mile of them; and there Paudeen and Flick rested blissfully until the morning.

IV

The Hare and the Donkey were early afoot for the crossing of Slieve League. First they followed the course of the swift Glen river for a mile or two; then they climbed by a mountain road, winding ever upward until they had left behind them the last thatched cottages snuggled in a dip of the land; soon the fields faded out against the mountain-side with the golden gorse encroaching on their borders. Past the lonely Lough O'Mulligan the road dwindled into a track and eventually petered out on the windy plateau of Bunglass.

"Are you sure you can find the way?" asked Paudeen.

"Of course I can!" cried Flick. "Sure, I know this whole mountain like the back of my paw. There's a second cousin of mine over there. Hey, Rolfe!"

The Hare addressed as Rolfe stopped and stared at Flick for a few seconds, then recognition dawned, and he came bounding over to greet him. Somehow he must have contrived to pass the word along the mountain that Flick was there, for more and more hares kept popping up from behind every tuft and boulder to say

"How d'ye do," and be introduced to Paudeen—hares called Slipper and Lep and Pat and Flash, and Clara and Bets, and little leverets with names like Scamp and Scurry. Why, thought Paudeen, this is like a royal procession. No wonder Flick wanted to come over Slieve League!

A small delegation accompanied them as far as a place they called the 'great view,' where the biggest and fattest Hare bade them good-bye in a neat little speech in which he expressed the hope that Paudeen's shadow might never grow less, and referred to Flick (greatly to his delight) as an intrepid explorer. Then Flick's friends turned back, leaving himself and the Donkey on their own again.

"Come over to the edge, Paudeen," called Flick, "and take a good long look, for yonder's the highest cliff in Ireland, and here's where you get the best view of it. Isn't it wonderful? Did you ever imagine anything so grand?"

Taking care not to tread too near the edge, Paudeen leaned forward and gazed, speechless with admiration and awe. There ahead of them sloped the massive cliff-face, two thousand feet of it, brown and purple and russet and ochre and green, looking as though a painter's colours had spilled over and run riotously into one another. The boulders on the shore far beneath seemed tiny as gravel, and the mighty Atlantic rollers surging in were dwarfed to ripples. A boisterous wind tore across the cliff-top, roaring in their ears.

"It's magnificent—like standing on the edge of the world," said Paudeen at last.

"That's what it is," answered Flick. "Next stop, America!" He gazed reflectively across the expanse of ocean and added, "I wish I had a song for this place,

Paudeen, but it's too big for me; my poor little songs can't match Slieve League."

"I don't suppose anybody else's could either," declared Paudeen loyally. "Oh, but I'm glad you brought me here, Flick! This will be something for me to remember all my life long."

"And now to cross the One Man's Path," said Flick, swinging round suddenly and leading the way on the next stage of their journey. "Here's where you'll need a steady head, Paudeen!"

"I'm ready for anything," responded Paudeen, gallantly plodding after him. "That rest we had under the bridge did me a power of good. Sure, I've climbed all this way, and I haven't sat down once!"

"Indeed, you're doing rightly," laughed the Hare. "Who knows, Paudeen, but I might have made a Punchestown winner out of you if I'd caught you a bit younger!"

The climb became stiffer at this point, and they had to save their breath for that; presently the cliff-edge shrank to a narrow ridge of stone running steeply upward. On the landward side the ground fell away abruptly to a dark mountain tarn; on the seaward there was a precipice; and in between stretched the two-foot-wide, dizzy pathway that pointed to the summit.

"The One Man's Path!" cried Flick, with as much pride as if he had invented it.

The Donkey contemplated it with deep misgiving. "If only the wind would drop for a moment!" he said.

"Try to get across between the gusts of wind," Flick advised him. "Look, I'll show you."

He ran lightly across and back again to demonstrate how simple it was.

Paudeen plucked up his courage, risked a few steps,

hesitated half-way across, drew back, was caught by a buffet of wind, and suddenly decided to go on, completing the perilous passage in a burst of panic.

"Bravo!" shouted the Hare, enthusiastically clapping him on the back as they both stretched themselves out to recover. "Good old Paudeen—you're probably the only Donkey who's ever been across the One Man's Path, so that's something to brag about!"

"Who was the 'One Man'?" asked Paudeen, when he felt like talking again.

"The spirit of the mountain, maybe," said Flick. "Or it could be the faery king himself—he has a palace up here."

"Oh, where?" inquired Paudeen, surveying the landscape.

"It's a faery palace," Flick told him, "so you couldn't see it. Anyway, he's not here now, for the mountain's clear. When the faery king summons his council he wreaths the mountain round with mist so that mortal eyes can never witness the rites of the faeries."

"Dear me," said the Donkey, "and not a soul to know what they do be doing when they're hidden away like that on the top of Slieve League?"

"Not a one," said Flick. "The foolhardy folks who tried to find out never came back. The mountain swallowed them."

Before the two animals left their viewpoint and began the descent to Glencolumbkille the Hare took time to tell the Donkey the names of the mountains they could see on every side. To the north were the Derryveagh Mountains with the forked peak of Errigal catching the sun; to the east lay the Bluestack Mountains from which the Donkey had come; across Donegal Bay, in

E

Sligo, they could see the craggy face of Benbulben and the greater height of Truskmore; next came the Ox Mountains; and faintly distinguishable, on the south-west horizon, were Nephin and Slieve Car and the Mountains of Mayo.

The Hare showed him many other wonderful things, too, as they travelled on, things the Donkey had never had time to notice before, when he was working so hard—the delicate maidenhair fern, clinging to its crevice of rock; the sundew, catching and sucking in the flies; the *caenavaun* (or bog-cotton) that God sent when the lonely bogland prayed for a flower of its own; the hidden nest of a wheatear.

"I found some white bluebells here the last time I passed," said Flick. "Oh, and farther down there's a patch of hungry grass—be very careful not to step on it, Paudeen."

"What would it do to me?" asked the Donkey.

"Why, you'd die, surely," cried the Hare, "the very life sapped out of you by the hungry grass. They say that wherever some poor starving soul sank down and died during the great famine the spot is marked for ever after by a hunger on the grass that cannot be appeased. Even the human beings know about it and, going through the hills, carry a crust in their pocket for fear they tread unaware on the hungry grass."

"Salt sea-water that only makes us thirstier, and grass that is hungrier than we are! What strange world have you taken me into?" mused Paudeen.

"It's the same world," said Flick, "only you didn't know anything about it till now. It's a world worth wandering in, I tell you!"

The sun was low in the western sky when the two friends came down through flowery meadows into the

Leabarlanna Puiblide
Catrac Áta Cliat

peaceful, secluded valley of Glencolumbkille. The very first thing the Donkey did was to look for the stone cross of St Columcille that Cissie the Cow had told him of, and there in the sunset glow he knelt to pray. Flick did not need to ask what the Donkey's prayer was for; he knew as well as if he had heard every word of it.

When the Donkey raised his head he saw how the setting sun had sent a bright beam right across the valley and picked out one whitewashed cottage on the hill. By a trick of the light the other houses scattered through the valley were dimmed in shadow; only this one shone like a beacon, its windows flashing back the brilliance of the sun's rays.

"That's it!" cried the Donkey, excitedly getting to his feet. "See, Flick, how St Columcille is pointing it out to me! Can you take me there before darkness falls?"

"I'll try," promised Flick, and he led the way.

V

It was twilight by the time the Donkey reached the cottage on the hill, and Seumas Meehan was lighting the oil-lamp. On a stool by the turf-fire sat Maura, his wife, nursing the child that was racked with coughing. A queer kind of whooping-cough, she was thinking to herself, to be lasting from the rainy days of April right into the month of June, and little sign of its clearing yet. "A nervous reaction," the doctor called it, whatever that was—if, indeed, he knew himself. Sometimes Maura wondered if it was some kind of spell that had come upon them, but surely there was nobody in the valley who would wish harm to a six-year-old child the like of Sheelagh!

"Do you know what?" exclaimed her husband, as he

set the lamp on the windowsill. "There's a strange Donkey out in the paddock."

"Ach, you're seeing things!" said Maura wearily. "Where would a Donkey stray from, I ask you?"

"It's there, all the same," Seumas replied. "Look for yourself."

Sheelagh stirred and sat up in her mother's arms. "Let me see!" she cried. "I want to see the Donkey. Please let me see the Donkey!"

Her mother set her down, and she ran across to the window and climbed on a chair to look out. Just then the Donkey, cropping the turf, moved into a patch of shadow and was lost from view. Sheelagh flew to the door and would have been out had her mother not caught her.

"What are you thinking of," Maura scolded, "to run out barefoot at this time of night and you with scarcely a stitch on you—are you mad entirely?"

"I only wanted to look at the Donkey!" wailed Sheelagh, dragged back to the fire. In her excitement she had brought on another fit of coughing. The tears ran down her cheeks.

"Wheesht, now," said Seumas. "Give over your crying and I'll take you outside for a minute to look at the little Ass." He pulled a blanket off the bed and began to wrap the child up in it.

"Seumas," said Maura, in a queer, excited voice, laying her hand upon his arm as he busied himself with these preparations, "Seumas, do you know what I'm thinking? That the Donkey might have been sent to us for a purpose. You know what your Aunt Breslin said? 'Pass the child under a donkey,' she said, 'and you'll find she'll be as right as rain.' 'Tis a sure cure for the chin-cough,' she said, 'all on account of the blessed cross every donkey bears on his back——' "

"I know, I know," Seumas interrupted, "and who'd heed Aunt Breslin and her superstitions? There'll be no child of mine passed under a donkey, I'm telling you plain. I'm surprised at you, Maura."

"We've tried everything else," murmured Maura disconsolately. "Surely it wouldn't do any harm? Ah, well, never mind, maybe the Donkey will bring us luck without."

Hoisting the child in his arms, Seumas strode across the kitchen floor, his nailed boots making a scraping sound on the stones. Maura was waiting with her finger on the latch of the door. But the moment the three of them went outside the Donkey ran away.

"Poor little brute! He's very timid," said Seumas. Maura darted into the house and came back with an apple in her hand. "Here, little Ass," she called. "Did you ever get taste of an apple? Come here to me now."

Paudeen (for the Donkey was indeed Paudeen) would have liked the apple very much. He wished she would leave it on the ground for him and go away. Perhaps it was his long association with the Hare that had made him more suspicious of human contact than he used to be, for as the woman advanced the Donkey retreated, keeping his eyes all the while warily fixed on her.

"Ach, I've no time to be coaxing you," said Maura. "Take it or leave it." And, tossing the apple on the ground, she turned and went back into the house.

Paudeen stood with large mournful eyes and questioning ears and contemplated the apple; but he did not move.

"Let me!" pleaded the little girl, struggling in her father's arms. "Perhaps he'll take it from me."

"Careful, now," warned her father, as Sheelagh,

bending to pick up the fruit where it lay, tripped in the folds of the blanket she had clutched about her. "He's strange, mind; he doesn't know you."

"Take your supper, Donkey!"

Paudeen solemnly regarded the little figure that came stumbling across the grass towards him, and he found that he had no inclination to run. Why, she was smaller than he was! There was nothing to be afraid of with her.

"Dear, nice Donkey," she was murmuring, "Mother says you came to make me well. Did you? You look so wise, perhaps you *do* know how to chase my cough. Take your supper, Donkey!"

Paudeen reached forward, gently nuzzled her out-stretched hand, and accepted the apple. Sheelagh watched and listened, enraptured, as he crunched the fruit, closing his eyes so as to concentrate on enjoying the tart juices. When he had finished Sheelagh whis-pered something in his ear, and Paudeen nosed her hair and seemed to whisper back.

"He's used to childer, by the look of it," said Seumas, hovering tactfully in the background. "His supper's over, so come away to your bed now, like a good girl. You'll see him in the morning."

"You won't slip away during the night, will you?" Sheelagh anxiously asked the Donkey. "Oh, please don't go away! Promise!" And, twining her arms about his neck, she gave Paudeen a good hearty hug. The blanket fell unheeded from her shoulders to the ground.

"Do you want to catch your death of cold, child?" cried Seumas, hurrying forward to gather her up. The Donkey scuttled off into the darkness.

"He knows how to cure my chin-cough, anyhow," Sheelagh informed her father, as she was borne away in the direction of the house. "He's going to show me a place in the hills where I can bury it, and it'll never, never be heard again."

"Well, now, fancy that!" said Seumas. "Indeed, yon old Neddy wasn't behind the door the day they were giving out the brains."

"His name's not Neddy," Sheelagh corrected him, in a tone of mild reproof. "It's Paudeen—he told me so. And he's come so far, miles upon miles upon miles——"

The door closed behind them, cutting off their friendly voices, and Paudeen was alone again. He watched the door expectantly, and, sure enough, in a few moments Seumas reappeared, made his way to the barn, and returned with a bundle of straw which he spread on the floor of an open outhouse.

"There's a shelter for you if it rains," he called to Paudeen. "See, I'll leave the door open, so that you can go and come as you please—I know it's an unhappy feeling to be closed up. Good-night to you, little Ass, and God bless!"

As soon as Seumas had gone away Paudeen went into the shed to explore. It was an ideal place for a Donkey to sleep, warm and dry and comfortable, and as he lay down on the crisp, rustling straw Paudeen said to himself. "I'm in clover, I am! I'm on the pig's back now! And it's all thanks to St Columcille and the Hare. I wonder where Flick is now?"

A head popped round the doorway. "Hallo!" called a bright, familiar voice. "You're doing fine, aren't you, Paudeen? Are you for staying?"

"Oh, yes, I think so," answered Paudeen. "They've been very nice to me so far. But just in case I should ever want to change my mind, Flick, when will you be back this way?"

Flick considered the question, rubbing his nose as he usually did when he was thinking. "I have to see a friend in Ardara this week," he said, "and I'd like to go on to Glenties after that. Tell you what, Paudeen, I'll come and visit you at the next full moon (that will be in two weeks from now), and by then you'll have had time to decide whether you're settled or whether you want to move on. That do? Good! You'll excuse me, won't you? Must fly. Cheerio in the meantime, Paudeen, old chap. Look after yourself!"

As he heard the Hare's busy paws padding away into the darkness Paudeen stretched himself luxuriously on his straw and sighed in profound contentment. Thank goodness, he said to himself, to be finished—with wandering. No—more—travels—for Paudeen. He's staying—— The rest of the sentence disappeared in a yawn, and Paudeen had fallen fast asleep.

The following morning the Meehans were seated at their breakfast when Sheelagh suddenly said, "Here's the doctor!"

"What?" cried her mother, jumping to her feet. "At this hour—and me not cleaned nor tidied!"

Over the half-door appeared the long face of Paudeen, and Sheelagh and her father burst out laughing.

"Now, that was a start to give me!" said Maura reproachfully. "Are you sure you've finished your breakfast, Sheelagh?"

"Yes," said the little girl, driving her spoon through the bottom of the empty eggshell and clambering down from her chair. "I'll take a piece with me, though—no, two pieces, one with butter and rhubarb jam, and one with butter alone."

"Is one for the Donkey?" Maura questioned suspiciously.

Sheelagh nodded.

"With butter?" said her mother, in scandalized tones. "Such extravagance!"

"Ach, Maura, the doctor's surely entitled to his fee," put in Seumas. "He must be a good one, too, for not a cough have I heard out of that child since the moment he came. He's brought us good luck, and no mistake!"

So Paudeen got his buttered piece after all; and with her arm about his neck Sheelagh conducted him round the little farm and through the neighbouring fields, till an appetizing smell wafted from the cottage door drew them both home again.

"What are you baking, Mother?" said she, leaning her elbows on the half-door and gazing in. A hen flew up beside her, but Sheelagh promptly shooed it away.

"Soda farls," Maura replied, raising a face that was flushed from bending over the griddle swung above the turf-fire. "Don't tell me you're hungry again."

"I only want the wee faery one," said Sheelagh, "when you come to it."

"Fetch me some water from the rain barrel then," said her mother, reaching out a shining tin can.

"You see, Paudeen," Sheelagh explained, as she dipped the can into the barrel, "the wee faery bannock's only given as a reward for something you've done. It's the very last one, made with a hole through the middle so that the faeries won't charm the baking; and it tastes the nicest of the lot."

When Sheelagh got her reward she straightway presented it to Paudeen, for he had never even seen a faery bannock before.

"Dear, but you'll have that Donkey ruined," Maura scolded. "You're too set on him altogether. What'll you do when the authorities come and take him away?"

"Oh, they couldn't do that!" cried Sheelagh. "The Gardai couldn't take my Paudeen!" And she held him so tightly that the Donkey thought he would choke.

"He's bound to have an owner somewhere," Maura pointed out. "We can't keep other people's property."

"We could buy him, couldn't we?" said Sheelagh. In her fright at the thought of losing Paudeen she had begun to cough again.

Maura shrugged her shoulders. "Your father has enough to pay for without acquiring an Ass into the bargain," she said abruptly. Possibly she had never quite forgiven Paudeen for not trusting her in the first place.

For answer Sheelagh rushed into the kitchen, seized her money-box from the dresser, and ran down the hill to the field where her father was forking hay. At her heels cantered Paudeen.

"Of course you'll get keeping him, Sheelagh love," her father comforted her, when she told him the trouble she was in. "Don't cry, now, a stór, it'll be all right. I'll go and report to the Gardaí as soon as we've milked the cows in the evening, and that will keep us on the right side of the law. If nobody claims the Donkey within three months I'd say he should be ours anyhow; but if an owner does turn up I'll undertake to raise the wind somehow and find enough cash to buy him over. Put back your money-box now, and stop worrying, there's a good girl. Get him to show you the place where he's going to bury your cough."

Nobody ever claimed Paudeen, and so he stayed with the Meehans. Sheelagh and he became fast friends in the days that followed. One evening during a thunderstorm the little girl put on her waterproof and wellingtons and went out to spend the time in Paudeen's shed, lest he should grow nervous by himself.

"Don't be afraid, Paudeen," she whispered, stroking his ears as the thunder rumbled overhead. "It's only the people upstairs—the angels, you know—heaving the furniture about. They're late with their spring-cleaning this year." A momentary flash of lightning illuminated the scene. "There!" said Sheelagh. "What did I tell you? That was the light of heaven shining through a chink in the floorboards. Nothing to be frightened about! They're always up to something, the people upstairs—times they set the whole sky aflame, and times they do be shaking their featherbeds till the feathers come fluttering down all on top of us, little cold feathers that melt. But you wouldn't be afraid of that either, would you, Paudeen?"

By the next week Sheelagh was so much improved that she was able to go back to school, accompanied by Paudeen, who carried the schoolbag. The Donkey looked as if he would like to have gone into the classroom with her, but that was not allowed. After a day or two Paudeen was able to calculate when Sheelagh was due to return, and he would wander across the fields, his feet stained yellow with buttercups, on his way to meet her coming home. They usually took the short cut through the fields unless the grass was very wet, and Paudeen would always carry the schoolbag, and sometimes carry Sheelagh too if she were tired.

Then, on the night of the full moon, the Hare came back. Sheelagh (who should have been sound asleep) was looking out of the little window at the time, watching Paudeen as he moved about like a small ghost, nose to the grass. All of a sudden the bushes quivered, and a very lively Hare bounded on to the scene. Paudeen gave a little whine of joy and ran towards him. After they had greeted each other the two animals began to exchange their news.

"But aren't you tired of staying here by now?" inquired Flick. "How about a trip north for a change? The weather's still good."

"No, thank you very much," said the Donkey. "I've finished with wanderings, Flick. You see, I found the fortune I was always looking for, and it's right here."

"So you've quite made up your mind?" asked the Hare.

"Absolutely," declared Paudeen.

"A dance, then!" shouted Flick, jumping in the air. "Come on, Paudeen. You always said you'd dance in celebration once you'd found your fortune. You promised. I'll start you off." And, kicking up his paws, Flick began to sing at the top of his voice:

> The moon is shining bright, Paudeen—
>   Come, dance and sing!
> Let your heels go where they will
>   Do the highland fling!
> Try the sailor's hornpipe,
>   Dance a jig and reel;
> Let your feet go happy
>   When it's happy you feel!

The Hare dashed off round the turf, bouncing like a ball, till he landed back where he had started from. Inside the house Sheelagh's cries of delight had brought her father and mother to the window, and they all stood to watch the antics of the Hare.

"What a waste of energy!" sighed Maura.

"That's Paudeen's friend," whispered Sheelagh, "the Hare who guided him here. He told me." She clapped her hands in excitement. "Oh, look!" she cried. "Do look at Paudeen!"

"Well, I never witnessed the like of that before!" ejaculated Seumas. "Who would have believed it?"

Slowly, solemnly, the Donkey had begun to dance. Maybe it was a minuet that he was trying with his neat, dignified steps, or it could have been a pavane; but, whatever it was, Paudeen was undeniably dancing, dancing there in the moonlight from sheer happiness, as no donkey had ever danced before; dancing because his prayer had been answered, his dreams had all come true, and he had found his fortune!

5

The Rabbit and the Pine Marten

~~~~~~

Once upon a time the Rabbit, when returning from his travels, came through a fir-wood, dense and thick with undergrowth. He lolloped along quite happily for a bit, nibbling a little grass here and a little there, and then he lighted on a patch that seemed familiar. Sure enough, it bore the marks of his earlier nibblings half an hour before. That's funny, thought the Rabbit, and he turned to go back the way he had come. This time he ran along the woodland path without pausing for any wayside snacks—and in fifteen minutes he was back where he had started. "Oh, dear, oh, dear," said the Rabbit, "this wood is most confusing. I do wish I could find somebody to show me the way out of it!"

As if in answer to his prayer the Rabbit heard a rustling in the branches over his head and looked up to see a strange creature coming down the tree. He was a handsome fellow, with a long bushy tail and golden-brown coat, and the Rabbit had never seen anyone like him before. The Rabbit waited until he was almost at the ground before calling out in his friendly way, "Hallo there!" To his astonishment the strange animal jumped down from the tree and made for the undergrowth at top speed.

"Oh, please, please!" called the Rabbit, running after him. "I'm lost in your wood. Please help me and show me how to get home!"

The other animal hesitated, then turned and began to come towards the Rabbit, sniffing the air cautiously as he advanced.

He has a very intelligent face, thought the Rabbit, for all that he's scared. Rather like a stoat, though he has a look of Ruairi Fox, too. I wonder who he is?

Soon only a couple of yards of leaf-strewn path separated them.

"I'm sorry if I startled you——" the Rabbit began.

"Hush!" breathed the other, peering furtively into the shadows. "Not so loud! Once darkness falls I'll guide you out of the wood; till then you'd better come in here and hide." He led the way into the damp under-growth, wriggling through incredibly small openings that squeezed the breath out of the Rabbit, until eventu-ally they had landed themselves in an almost impene-trable nest of briars.

"I hope I don't lose all my fur getting out of here," the Rabbit remarked. "What are you so frightened of, anyway?"

"Men," whispered the strange animal, shivering in his golden-brown coat.

"My goodness! Is that all?" exclaimed the Rabbit. "Sure, any animal with half an ounce of sense can outwit a man!"

"They have snares and traps and guns," said the other.

"I know—and animals have keener eyes and ears and noses, and legs to run," replied the Rabbit.

"Running away wouldn't do me much good," sighed the woodland animal sadly. "If any man got a glimpse of me he wouldn't rest till I was captured or shot. I'm such a rare animal, you see, I wouldn't stand a chance of escape."

"Is that so?" cried the Rabbit. "Well, you do surprise me, for when the human beings try to catch us rabbits they say it's because there are too many of us! You wouldn't know what they wanted, would you?"

The other animal shook his head gloomily, and they sat for a little while in despondent silence; then the Rabbit brightened up and said, "No use worrying, anyway—let's think of something cheerful. You know, I do wish you'd tell me your name."

His companion took another uneasy glance to make sure no one was listening, then he whispered, "I'm a Pine Marten, called Marty for short. Extinct—officially."

"What do you mean—'extinct officially'?" demanded the Rabbit.

"Well, you never saw me before, did you?"

"No," the Rabbit admitted. "I thought I knew every animal tribe in Ireland, but I never met you till now. Mind you, I've heard my great-grandfather speak of the pine martens, but I didn't think there were any of them living here nowadays."

"Exactly," responded the Pine Marten. "There are so few of us left that most people think we have died out altogether. In other words, we're extinct, officially. So long as human beings believe that, we go unmolested and are relatively safe; that's why I'm forced to hide away in the woods and never, never show myself. You mustn't breathe a word about our meeting after you've gone back home—promise me."

"I'd like to tell my wife and one special friend," said the Rabbit, "but you needn't be afraid. I won't give away your hiding-place or say where I met you—cross my heart! I never got another animal into trouble in my life."

"Thank you, Coney," replied the Pine Marten.

The Rabbit's face gave a twinge. "Oh, please don't

call me by that old-fashioned name!" he implored. "Nobody does but the Fox. I've been known as 'Rabbit' for years and years now."

"I'm sorry," the Pine Marten apologized. "I believe I did hear something of the sort, but an extinct animal gets very out of touch with society, you know. Pray forgive me if I make blunders."

"Of course," said the Rabbit, "I quite understand." Meditatively he added, "It must be a very strange existence you lead, Marty, shut away by yourself, getting only occasional little trickles of information from the world outside. I couldn't endure that at all—I'd simply have to know what everybody was doing and what was going on!"

"Curiosity doesn't pay," observed the Pine Marten. "The curious animal gets caught; the wary animal lives long. Now, if you'll excuse me, Rabbit, I'll just take a peek outside to see if the coast's clear."

"I'll go," said the Rabbit at once.

"No, no," insisted the Pine Marten. "You stay here. You don't know the dangers of these woods."

The Rabbit sighed and resigned himself to wait. Soon he heard a voice calling softly, "Come on, Rabbit, it's a fine dark night, and there's nobody about."

Now to find my way out of this barbed-wire entanglement! muttered the Rabbit to himself, pulling at the briars and getting more involved every minute. The Pine Marten heard his squeaks of annoyance and slithered back through a hole to show the Rabbit the way out.

"Phew!" gasped the Rabbit, when he had struggled into the open again. "That was an experience! I've always been interested in finding out how other animals live, but I've come to the conclusion that a dry, sandy burrow like mine is hard to beat!"

F

"The top of a tree is the safest place," remarked the Pine Marten, helping the Rabbit to pick the thorns out of his fur. "Now, in which direction do you want to go?"

"North," replied the Rabbit. "County Antrim."

"This way, then," signalled the Pine Marten, and the pair of them started off.

At first they had to halt every few moments to allow the Pine Marten to listen and sniff the night air, but once he was satisfied that no danger offered itself he grew more confident and even talkative.

"You manage to keep up with everything that happens, I suppose?" he asked the Rabbit.

"Oh, yes," the Rabbit beamed. "I pride myself on being well informed."

"Tell me this, then," said the Pine Marten, laying a friendly paw on the Rabbit's shoulder as they walked along together, "what is Dean Swift writing these days? I liked his book about the horses—you know, the one where Gulliver journeys to a land which is ruled by horses, with men as their slaves. That was a good story!"

"I'm afraid it rather belongs to the past," the Rabbit explained. "You see, Marty, it's two hundred years or more since Dean Swift was alive."

The Pine Marten shook his head in sad concern. "Dear, oh, dear, what an old fogey you must think me," he sighed. "It's so difficult for an extinct animal to keep in touch with events—why, I must be years behind the times! And my old friend Dick Martin of Ballynahinch Castle, he whom we called 'Humanity Martin' because he was such a good friend to all us animals—is he dead too?"

The Rabbit nodded. "I'm afraid so. But look, Marty, let me be your friend. I'll come back and talk to you some other day and give you all the news of the last two hundred years, shall I?"

"No, no," said the Pine Marten, "it's very kind of you, Rabbit, but please don't trouble. You must understand what it means to be an extinct animal; you'll never be able to find me again, no matter how hard you try. If you come here I'll be Elsewhere; and if you go there I'll be Some Other Place. So you see, it's no use."

"I'm sorry about that," said the Rabbit. "I'd like to meet you again, Marty."

"Hush," whispered the Pine Marten, "we must be getting near the outskirts of the wood now, so tread as softly as you can."

A long-drawn, eerie *whoo-ooh!* sounded from the thicket behind them, and the Pine Marten instantly froze in his tracks. "Only an owl," observed the Rabbit unconcernedly, as he bobbed along.

Without further alarm the two animals arrived at the edge of the wood; there was no moon, but in the dim light shed by the stars the Pine Marten's creamy waistcoat gleamed and the white tuft on the end of the Rabbit's tail shone every time he bobbed.

"Perhaps you ought to go back now," said the Rabbit considerately.

"I was just about to give you a few directions," the Pine Marten replied, "when I suddenly remembered another question I wanted to ask. Tell me this, Rabbit, and tell me no more—has the Loch Ness Monster been stirring lately?"

The Rabbit was almost too astonished to reply.

"Y-yes," he stammered, "the Monster's been seen any number of times in the last fifteen or twenty years—but, Marty dear, how on earth did you, living in the past the way you do, ever get to hear about him?"

The Pine Marten looked at the Rabbit reproachfully. "Come, come," he said, "the Loch Ness Monster was mentioned by St Adamnan in the seventh century. I'm surprised at you, Rabbit, not knowing that. Look it up when you get home!"

"I will," promised the Rabbit. "That's certainly something I never knew before."

"Now," said the Pine Marten, "I can show you your way from here. That clump of trees is due north from where we're standing. Can you make out a hill over there with a cairn of stones on the top? Keep it always on your right and you can't lose yourself. You'll find there's a path that winds round the foot of the hill and crosses the river by a wooden bridge. Not far beyond the bridge you'll come to the main road leading to Belfast. Good luck, Rabbit, and safe home!"

When the Rabbit turned from studying the clump of trees, the cairn of stones, and the hill, it was to find that the Pine Marten had vanished.

"Oh, dear, and I never even thanked him!" muttered the Rabbit, annoyed with himself. He strained his eyes to look back, but there wasn't a sight or a sound of Marty anywhere. He was a strange creature, the Rabbit reflected, as he set out on his long journey northward, but I did like him. Poor old Marty! I must come back and talk to him one day.

But though the Rabbit has tried his hardest he has never been able to find the Pine Marten again, not in the fir-wood, nor anywhere else.

"It's like a dream," says the Rabbit, "but it can't have been a dream, because I did look it up, and, do you know, the Pine Marten was quite right about the Loch Ness Monster!"

6

What happened when the Pig found a Penny

∞∞∞∞∞∞∞∞∞∞∞∞∞∞∞∞∞∞∞∞∞∞∞∞∞∞∞∞

The trouble all started when the Pig on Mulligans' farm found a penny. He was rootling about under the apple-trees, hoping for early windfalls, when he came on the penny and wondered what it was.

"That's money," said the Dog. (The Dog knew quite well, for he had often gone with the children to the shop to help fetch home the messages.) "You put that away and keep it carefully," he advised the Pig. "You never know when you may need money."

"I've nowhere to put it till I'm back in my sty," said the Pig. "Would you look after it for me, Spot?"

"Surely," agreed the Dog, and he took the penny in his mouth and hid it in at the back of his kennel. Then he went down into the orchard with the Pig to see if they could find any more money. Before long they had discovered another two pennies and a halfpenny, for there was a hole in Michael Mulligan's pocket, though they did not know that then. The Pig was thrilled when he saw the halfpenny.

"Look!" he cried. "Look, Spot, there's a pig on it!¹ Well, bless my stars, if it isn't my old friend Sally Grumphie! I knew her when we were piglets. She won a lot of prizes at shows when she grew up—her

¹ The Irish coins show an animal on one side.

photograph used to be in all the papers. Quite a beauty-queen, was Sally. She married a large white boar, I be-lieve—but anyhow, there she is with her family. Isn't it a small world, Spot?"

Spot, not being particularly interested in the Pig's acquaintances, barely disguised a yawn. Then suddenly his attention was caught by the sight of three hens scratching vigorously on the ground and clucking in excitement, and he wandered over to investigate. The hens had found a threepenny-bit. They did not know what it was, either; in fact, they thought it was a bean, and were trying to break it with their beaks when the Dog came and took it from them and carried it to his kennel. Clucking and scolding, the hens followed him, and the Dog had to explain to them what money was and how the human beings made use of it. He told them to bring in all they could find, and when there was enough he would organize a feast for the whole farm-yard.

At the mention of food the hens went to work with a will, pecking and peering and scratching the earth, and before dusk fell they had brought in three more pennies and deposited them with the Dog for safe keeping. The news soon spread, and next day all the animals and fowl could be seen, noses and beaks to the ground, searching for the coins that were scattered so mys-teriously here and there over the farm. The luckiest one that day was Prince, the Horse, who found a shilling when he was out carting hay. By the end of the second day there was a total of one-and-ninepence-halfpenny in the animals' bank.

Then the Dog began to feel the weight of respon-sibility growing too heavy for him. "I'm scared to take my eyes off that kennel," he confided to the Horse.

"Wouldn't it be dreadful if anybody stole the animals' money? What should I do?"

"We'll get the Rabbit to hide it in his burrow," suggested the Horse. "He's a very reliable chap. Hey, Rabbit! Rabbit!"

A head perked up from behind a tuft of grass, and next moment the Rabbit came into the farmyard, running. He felt tremendously important when he was told what he had to do.

"Gosh!" he said. "A real bank—and I'll be the banker in charge of all the money stowed away in the vaults! I'll enjoy that."

"You must be very, very careful, remember," the Horse admonished him. "We know exactly how much there is, so don't you allow any of your little bunnies to play with it or lose it."

"Certainly not," said the Rabbit, offended. "Do you think I have no professional pride?"

The Dog came out of the house with an empty brown sugar-bag in his mouth, and together the three friends, watched by the Pig and a few hens, counted the coins into the bag, and the Rabbit took them away.

On the third day only one penny was brought in— carried proudly in the broad beak of a duck, while all her friends marched in a procession behind her. She had dredged it up from the mud at the side of the pond: the penny was green and discoloured, and the hens regarded it very critically.

"Why, it's got a man's head on it!" exclaimed one hen. "If it was a genuine penny it would have a hen and chickens. It's no good, Quack."

"All right," said the duck, insulted. "If you don't want it——" and she prepared to scoop it up in her beak again.

But the Dog was too quick for her. "Hey, none of that!" he barked. "It's a perfectly good penny, only it's an old one that has been lying in the pond for years. Give it to me, Quack." And so that penny too was added to the little store in the Rabbit's burrow.

After the third day no more money was found, for by that time Granny Mulligan had discovered and mended the hole in the pocket of Michael's breeches.

On the fifth night of the new moon the Horse and Dog called a meeting to discuss how the money should be used. Lots of animals came who had had nothing whatever to do with the finding of the money; but that's the way of the world—they all turn up for the spending of it. When they were all gathered the Rabbit fetched the sugar-bag and emptied the contents on the turf for them to see. Immediately the Hare clapped his paw on the threepenny-bit.

"Mine!" he cried.

"Don't talk nonsense," said the Rabbit, trying to push him away. "You didn't find any. How could it be yours?"

"Doesn't matter," said the Hare. "It's got my picture on it, so it's mine."

"Then six of the pennies belong to us!" shrieked the hens.

"And my husband can claim the shilling," lowed the Cow.

"Look here," the Horse protested, "this is ridiculous. You should be able to see at a glance, Flick, that a model hare posed for that portrait. It's not you at all. If anybody was going to claim the money for himself it should be the one who found it; but although I found more than all the rest of you put together, I'm willing to share and share alike."

"That's right," cried the other animals (especially those who had not found anything). "Share and share alike."

The Hare reluctantly took his paw off the threepenny-bit, whereupon the Rabbit, with an indignant sniff, replaced the coin alongside the others and stood a little nearer in case there would be any more raids on the bank.

"Now, Spot," said the Horse, "tell us what human beings do with money. You should know the procedure."

"They buy tea and sugar and sometimes bread in the shop," replied the Dog. "It's quite simple. They just ask for what they want and hand over the money in exchange."

"Such an easy way to live!" sighed the Stoat, who often went hungry.

"They have to find the money first," the Horse reminded him, "and we must admit how tiresome that can be. Go on, Spot!"

"Well," continued Spot, "if I went into the shop by myself the old woman would probably first count the money in the bag, then she'd hold up everything in turn until I barked to tell her the right one, and then she'd parcel that up and give it to me. She's not very quick at dog-language, but I'd make her understand."

The animals looked dubious, and the Horse shook his head.

"Too risky," he decided. "We'll have to think of a better way. Why, you might come home with face-powder or tobacco or dear knows what."

"What's 'dear knows what'?" whispered the Hare in the Rabbit's ear.

"Dandelions," said the Rabbit, who could not be bothered answering the Hare's questions.

The Hare gave a great hoot of laughter which he instantly smothered with his paw when the others turned and looked at him; but to this day the Hare is convinced that human beings go into the shop to buy dandelions, and he laughs every time he thinks of it. (It doesn't take much to make a hare laugh.)

"I could get Micky Mulligan to write me a note," the Dog suggested. "He's started school two years past."

"Fine! That would be *much* better!" said the Horse. "Now to the main business. I take it we're all agreed that we shall spend our money on food?"

Above the chorus of eager, assenting voices could be heard the bleat of the Sheep.

"The money doesn't belong to us," she objected. "It's our duty to seek out the owner and return it to him."

"Finding's keepings," snapped the Goat. "You're always a wet blanket, Agnes."

"It would be very difficult for us to discover the owner, Agnes, my dear," said the Horse, in a more kindly tone. "For all we know, since there are ten coins there may be ten owners. Besides, the sum of money is quite small where human beings are concerned. The Dog tells me that the average man would never miss one-and-tenpence-halfpenny."

A murmur of wonder rose from the other creatures gathered round.

"I'm glad you mentioned that, Prince," the Dog put in, "because I think the animals are expecting too much for their money. It won't buy a lot, you know. There'll be hardly enough of anything to go round."

The animals looked sadly at the little pile of coins gleaming in the starlight. It was their treasure, their all;

and now they seemed to see it shrinking before their very eyes!

But Agnes the Sheep was still dissatisfied. "If we cannot find an owner for the money let us take it to the priest," she suggested. "It would be a sin to spend it on ourselves. The money is not ours."

At this the Goat lost his temper. "And it's not his either!" he shouted. "Really, Agnes, you make me sick. You must have a path worn to the chapel door by this time. If there's any animal that can raise the devil in me it's you, with your goody-goody ways."

"Hush! Hush!" cried the Horse in alarm. "Puck, do you want to waken the whole farmhouse? For any sake stop shouting! And that's no way to talk to Agnes, you heathen."

"It's all right, Prince, I'll go away," said the Sheep. "You'll have more freedom to do as you like with the money when I'm gone." And she walked with a dignified step out of the farmyard and up the hill beyond, out of sight. Some of the more sensitive animals looked uneasily at one another and felt a little ashamed.

"Good riddance!" ejaculated the Goat. "Now, back to business. What are we going to buy?"

The Cow gazed sadly after the Sheep. She would like to have gone with Agnes, who was her friend; but she badly wanted to be in at the animals' feast too, so in the end she stifled the twinges of conscience and pushed herself nearer to hear what they were discussing.

"I like tasty things myself," the Dog was saying, "but I quite realize that every animal can't digest the food I can. Similarly Prince (who is the largest shareholder in our company, remember) would have liked oats, but that wouldn't please the rest, either. The problem is to find something that every one can eat, which won't cost more than one-and-tenpence-half-penny and will go a long way. The Horse and I propose biscuits, plain biscuits, the kind human beings have. Broken biscuits work out cheaper, and I can easily knock over a tin next time I'm in the shop. We'd get a pound of those for our money. Would that suit everybody?"

The Donkey and Pig and Goat and Rat all voted for biscuit, and the Mouse and hens for biscuit-crumbs.

"Is biscuit like cattle-cake?" asked the Cow.

"It is, rather," said the Dog, "but more refined."

"All right," agreed the Cow, "I'd like that."

The Hare nudged the Rabbit. "Do you know anything about this—this—'bistick,' or whatever they call it?"

"No," whispered the Rabbit, "but don't let's show our ignorance." So they put up their paws and voted for biscuit too.

"Is everybody agreed, then?" called out the Dog. "One pound of plain biscuits to be brought from the shop and divided out evenly—or as evenly as we can manage—among the animals."

"Hurrah!" shouted all the animals in a chorus.

Then from the outskirts of the crowd came a loud, angry miaow in a voice they all knew well. The Cat had just arrived.

Into the centre of the ring she walked, as bold as a gipsy, and said jeeringly, "Biscuits! Just what a dog *would* think of! No imagination. Who wants biscuits, anyway?"

"We do," shouted the other animals in unison.

The Cat arched her back and wrinkled up her dainty little nose.

"Biscuits! Hard, dry, tasteless things!" she said, with all the contempt she could muster. "Well, I won't have it. I exercise my power of veto. I vote against biscuits."

Consternation broke out among the animals, who now saw themselves deprived of their feast at the whim of the Cat.

"You can't do that!" they cried.

"It's done in the highest political circles," remarked the Cat.

"There's a majority in favour of biscuits," snarled the Dog.

"But it's not unanimous," replied the Cat suavely, sitting down and beginning to lick her paw.

The Dog made a sudden angry dart in her direction, but the Horse put out a restraining hoof.

"Let me settle this diplomatically," he murmured. "You know, Kitty"—he turned to the Cat—"it may be forgetful of me, but I don't seem to remember your contributing any money to the animals' fund. Did you?"

"I have a vote just the same," retorted the Cat. "How much did the Donkey give you? Or the Cow? Or the Goat?"

"They all searched for money," said the Dog. "They hunted everywhere. What did you do?"

The Cat smiled disdainfully as she licked the other paw and proceeded to smooth her whiskers.

"You don't know what money is, you silly animals," she declared. "I could buy and sell the whole lot of you."

"Don't believe her!" growled the Dog. "She's deceitful, like all her tribe—disgusting animals, washing themselves in public!"

The Cat paused with paw upraised in the middle of a lick.

"Who's talking about washing?" she sneered.

"Poor old Spot! When does he ever have a bath? Twice a year, when he's thrown in the sheep-dip!"

It took the Horse and Cow and Donkey all their time to hold the Dog back when the Cat said that to him. He was furious. If he could have got near the Cat she would have felt the sharp nip of his teeth for her impudence—though of course Kitty had been wise enough to provoke him only when she knew she was well protected.

"Hush!" cried the Horse again. "Will you animals never cease from quarrelling? If you have any money, Kitty, go and get it."

"Very well," said the Cat, and she minced off in the direction of the house, without even troubling to hurry.

By and by the Cat reappeared, not carrying a coin in her mouth, as they had expected, but dragging after her a long dark object so heavy that it left a trail behind it in the grass. When she came nearer they could see that it was a black woollen sock, packed tight with money; the hard edges of the coins showed through, but so closely were they crammed into the sock that they did not even clink.

"It's a fortune!" gasped the Cow.

"We'll all be able to retire!" said the Horse.

"Hurrah! Hurrah!" shouted the others. "Long live the Cat!"

The Cat basked in their approving glances and purred with self-satisfaction. But her triumph was short-lived, for suddenly the Dog snarled and showed his teeth.

"She stole it!" he barked.

"I did not!" screamed the Cat, flying at him. "I found it!"

Again the Horse had to intervene hurriedly to keep the peace. "You animals will have me demented," he said. "Couldn't you be agreeable for a change?"

"Indeed, I never remember so much bad feeling before," remarked the Pig. "I'm beginning to be sorry I ever took that penny under my notice. I should have buried it."

"He called me a thief," mewed the Cat sulkily.

"And so she is," maintained the Dog, appealing to the others. "Anything we found we came by honestly, but the Cat stole that money. Didn't you see her coming straight from the house with it? It's old Granny Mulligan's savings, that's what it is."

The Cat was silent.

"If that's so you'd best leave it back where you got it, Kitty," said the Horse regretfully, as he picked up the sock in his mouth. "Come, now, like a good Cat, and show me where it was." He was an honest beast, but he could not help feeling sad at the thought that now he would not be able to retire after all, but must go on pulling the plough and the harrow, the reaper and binder, and the heavy old farm-cart with its iron-rimmed wheels.

Spot waited until the Horse had rejoined the group. The Cat did not return.

"Well," said Spot, "we've still got our original one-and-tenpence-halfpenny. Shall I buy the biscuits to-morrow?"

There was silence for a few moments, then the small voice of Lochag Mouse was heard. "It's true what the Pig said just now," squeaked the Mouse, "that finding this money has only made the animals greedy and quarrelsome and dishonest. If human money can do that to decent animals what effect would human biscuits have? Why, they might poison us altogether. For myself, I don't want any."

"I agree with Lochag," said the Pig. "We animals aren't meant to have money. Let's get rid of it."

"It's unlucky," declared the Rat, a superstitious animal. "Throw it away."

"I'd prefer to give it to a human being," said the Horse, "especially as they think so much of it."

The rest agreed with him.

"Just as you say," assented the Dog. "Do you approve, Banker Rabbit?"

The Rabbit bobbed and smiled and rubbed his front paws together as though he were washing them. "Certainly, certainly," he beamed. "Just as my clients decide! I am but the servant of the public—the humble servant of the public."

"Cut it out, Coney Rabbit!" snapped the Fox. Slinking unobserved into the back row of animals, Ruairi had waited to hear when the biscuits were to be given out, and now he was mad at himself, having lost a whole night's hunting for nothing. He would like to have gone round and boxed everybody's ears, starting with the Rabbit, but there were too many of them, and big animals like the Horse and Cow would stand no nonsense from a fox.

Next day the Dog set out to find some one to whom the animals could present the handsome sum of one-and-tenpence-halfpenny. (He left out old Granny Mulligan, for he considered her to be rich enough already.)

First he went to Michael Mulligan, who worked the farm. Michael was harnessing the Horse at the time.

"What would you do if you had money?" the Dog inquired.

"Buy a tractor," said Michael, without a moment's hesitation.

"Eh? And put me out of business?" cried Prince from between the shafts. "Don't give it to him, Spot!"

So Spot went on into the dairy, where Michael's wife Kathleen was busy churning with an old-fashioned churn. She was hot and breathless with the exertion of lifting and pushing the heavy plunger, and out of temper because the butter wouldn't come.

"What would you do if you got some money you didn't expect?" asked Spot.

"Do? I'd be off to America on the first boat," said Kathleen.

"Ah, sure, you wouldn't have the heart to go and leave us all!" said Spot. "Tell me, Kathleen, truthfully —what would you do?"

"Get this place electrified, for a start," answered Kathleen. "Now, out of my road, Spot!"

"And next thing, I suppose, you'd have the poor little chickens coming out of machines instead of being properly looked after by their mothers?" cried Spot indignantly, moving to the door. "Oh, no, we couldn't have that!"

He tackled young Micky next, when the little boy was bringing in an armful of turf for the kitchen fire and stacking it on the hearth under the direction of his granny.

"What would you like me to buy you?" the Dog whispered in his ear.

"Have you money, Spot?" asked Micky.

"A little," said the Dog.

"Oh, but I'd love a model aeroplane!" sighed Micky. "One that would really fly."

"Ach, I couldn't afford that," said Spot. "You want too much. If you had said a handful of toffees, now, or a couple of bars of chocolate, I might have managed it. I'll ask your little sister instead. Noreen, love, what would you like old Spot to bring you from the Longford

G

fair? A stick of rock, maybe, or some coloured pencils, or a bunch of ribbons for your hair?"

"No," said Noreen, "I want a walkie-talkie doll like Eileen Brady's. Will you buy me one, Spot?"

"I will not, then," the Dog replied crossly. "I haven't enough money for the like of that. You're all far too greedy, so you are."

He was about to sail out of the kitchen in the huff when Granny Mulligan suddenly leaned forward from her corner and pounced on him.

"Where did you hide your baggie, Spot?" she screeched. "I'd like fine to see what's in yon baggie! Come on, now, where did you put it?" And she shook him by the scruff of the neck till Spot's teeth rattled in his head and he growled.

"Stop it, Granny! You're hurting him!" Noreen wailed, trying to pull the old woman's hands away.

The moment her grip relaxed Spot squirmed free and was out of the door in a flash. His one thought was that he must get rid of that money quickly, or it would find its way into Granny Mulligan's sock with all the rest.

Off he sped to find his friend Prince. The Horse was having his mid-morning snack of hay when the Dog arrived, panting.

"Well, how did you get on?" inquired Prince, between mouthfuls. "You look very hot and bothered."

The Dog explained his predicament. "You should just have heard the style of the things they asked for!" he exclaimed. "Wouldn't you think the children, at least, might have welcomed a few toffees? But no, not they! I tell you, those human beings wouldn't be satisfied with less than a fortune apiece!"

"That's too bad," said Prince sympathetically, "but listen, I have a suggestion to make. There's an old

Caṫṙaċ Ṡċa Ċuaṡ

travelling woman out on the road beyond (I saw her when I was coming in from the top field) and I'm thinking by the looks of her she's so poor she'd be glad of any help we could give her. Try her with a little at a time, Spot, and see how she responds."

The Dog trotted off down the road at a brisk pace, till just past the turn he came on what appeared to be a bundle of old clothes in the hedge. He tiptoed over and, sniffing cautiously, assured himself that there really was an old woman inside. Then he sat down and waited for her to waken. By and by she grunted and stirred, and out of the cocoon of rags came a face, brown and wrinkled as a walnut.

"Hullo!" she said. "You're a nice dog!"

Spot waved his tail in approval.

"I've always been fond of a collie dog," mused the old woman, "though I've never had one of my own. Still, every dog in the county is my friend, so I'm not so badly off, am I?"

Spot came closer, and she fondled his head with a bony hand that was like the twisted root of a tree.

The Dog gazed up in her face. He liked her. "I have a little money to give away," he confided. "Could you use it?"

To his surprise the old woman cackled with laughter. "What would an old body like me do with money?" she asked him. "Maybe you're thinking I'd be planning to buy myself a silk gown to dance at the *ceilidhe* up in Ballymore—is that it? Or was it a few packets of cigarettes you had in mind for me?" And she laughed more than ever.

"Isn't there *anything* you want?" asked Spot, quite taken aback.

"Sure, I get my bite and sup from the people in the

houses round about," said the old woman, "and the farmers all know me and don't mind me sleeping a night in their barn or hay-loft. Times I do be joining up with other travelling people—tinkers, and the like—but mostly I do be going my lone. I'm not in need of anything, thanks be to God, unless perhaps——" Her voice trailed away.

She fondled his head with a bony hand

"Yes?" put in the Dog eagerly.

"I hardly like to ask you," the old woman went on, "but if you ever had threepence to spare maybe I could get Michael Mulligan——"

"That's my master!" interrupted the Dog in his excitement.

"Is he, then? That's how you're such a nice Dog! Well, I'd get Mike to write a letter to my son Cathal out in England, to ask him when he'll be coming home.

As soon as he would have enough money saved he was for buying a cottage on a little strip of land beside a river, just for him and me. We had it all planned, so we had—but dear, oh, dear, I haven't heard word of him for many's the long day. I don't think he'd be forgetting his old mother—it wouldn't be in him to do that—but, moving over the countryside the way I do, nobody knows for certain where I be. But I'll tell Cathal to write to me at Michael Mulligan's, for I'll be back this road twice before Lammas-tide. I could do that if only I had the money for the stamp."

Away went Spot, overjoyed, to his secret hidey-hole in the ditch, and came rushing back with the sugar-bag in his mouth. Carefully he emptied it at the old woman's feet. Out of it rolled the threepenny-piece with the hare on it, the shilling the Horse had found, seven pennies (including the duck's green one), and the halfpenny the Pig admired so much.

"This is never all for me?" cried the old woman incredulously. "Sure, it's far too much!"

"It's for you," Spot assured her. "A present from the animals. And now, before I go, tell me how you plan to spend the rest of it, for they'll be sure to ask."

"You've set me a bit of a problem, so you have," smiled the old woman, "giving me one-and-tenpence-ha'penny all of a sudden to throw round me, me that's not used to riches!"

"Anyhow, this will buy you the stamp," said Spot helpfully, putting aside the threepenny-piece.

"And this," added the old woman, lifting the shilling, "is for the chapel. It will be fine to have a respectable contribution for once."

I must remember to tell the Sheep about that, Spot said to himself.

The old woman reflected for a few moments. "Now, how much have we left?" she pondered. "One, two, three, four, five, six, seven pennies. Do you know, I think I'll go down to the shop and blow the whole lot on a bag of peppermint creams! It's years since I tasted one, and I used to be terrible fond of them. Would you come along with me and get share?"

"No, thank you all the same," said Spot. "Peppermints don't agree with me; they burn my tongue. I'll be going back now to tell the Horse I found you."

"Wait a minute," called the old woman, as she gathered up the money into the sugar-bag. "I'd like to give you something for yourself, you're such a nice Dog. Would you ever take back the ha'penny as a remembrance? And tell the animals they've made a poor old body feel like a queen this day!"

The Dog came over close to her and she put the halfpenny in his mouth. Then she bent down and pressed her lips to the white spot on the top of his head.

"I'll be seeing you by and by," she said. "When I come to get Michael Mulligan to write that letter for me I'll not forget to let him know what a good Dog he has!"

"You won't mention the money?" queried the Dog, with an anxious frown, dropping his coin to ask the question.

"No fear of me!" chuckled the old woman. "You don't come to my time of life without learning how to keep a secret, I'll tell you that!"

Spot stood watching till she had hobbled round the bend of the road, out of sight; then he turned and trotted back to the farmyard.

Maybe you're wondering what the Dog did with the halfpenny? Well, being a very unselfish Dog, he went straight to the Pig with it.

"Just take a look at what I've got for you, Pig," he called, standing up on his back paws to look down into the pigsty where the Pig was at the time. Then he dropped the halfpenny.

"Ee-ee-ee!" squeaked the Pig ecstatically. "It's Sally Grumphie! Ah, Sally Grumphie, my pin-up girl! Oh, thank you! Can I really keep it, Spot?"

"Really, truly," said Spot, his eyes twinkling. And he told the Pig how he had sought for some one who would be grateful for the animals' money, till at last he had found the old woman, and how in the end she had given him back the halfpenny to do as he liked with it.

So it came about that the Pig, who had found the first coin, got the last one to keep.

"Have you anywhere to put it?" asked Spot.

"Indeed, I'll find a safe place," replied the Pig, and he demonstrated how he could push it with his nose into a chink between the stones of the whitewashed wall in his sty.

"Good-bye now," said Spot, dropping on to all fours again, for his back legs were growing tired.

" 'Bye, Spot, and many, many thanks," called the Pig.

When the Dog had gone the Pig took out the halfpenny again, gazed at it in rapture, and imprinted on it a damp piggy kiss.

Maybe we'll meet again some day, Sally, my dear, he mused. Who knows, perhaps you'll be next to me in the spring show!

He smiled to himself at the thought, and his little eyes grew moist with sentiment, for even pigs have dreams.

7

How the Rabbit took a Ride

~~~~~~

Once upon a time the Rabbit went to visit some relatives of his who lived near Drogheda. As the Rabbit always wanted to see everything that was to be seen, the first day his friends took him to explore the subterranean chambers at Newgrange, and the second day to examine the animal carvings on the High Cross at Monasterboice, and the third to admire the wide sweep of the river Boyne below the railway bridge. When he got to the Boyne the Rabbit just sat back on his haunches and stared—not at the wide, slow river, nor at the viaduct that spanned it, nor even at the train puffing its way across, but at a double line of little buckets suspended from a cable and moving slowly against the sky.

For a while he watched, fascinated, then he turned to Brownie, the eldest of the Drogheda rabbits.

"You never said a word about this. What is it?" he asked.

Brownie, delighted to be able to tell his cousin from the North something he didn't know already, proceeded to explain.

"Why, those are the cement buckets," he replied. "Look, do you see the cement works down yonder, the big white place with the chimneys?"

The Rabbit nodded.

"That's where the buckets on this side are going, taking down stones from the quarry. You can't see the quarry from here, but it's about a couple of miles up that way."

He pointed with his paw, and the Rabbit nodded again.

"The buckets on the far side are the empty ones going back to the quarry for more stones," Brownie concluded. "That's all there is to it."

"But it's wonderful!" exclaimed the Rabbit, quite captivated, clasping his front paws together as he often did in moments of emotion. "I simply *must* have a ride in one of those little buckets! Have you often been up in one?"

"Certainly not!" exclaimed Brownie, to whom the idea had never even occurred. "What would I be doing that for?"

"Well!" cried the Rabbit, with a great show of indignation. "Here's a marvellous aerial railway at your very door, and you neglect your opportunities in such a fashion! I've a good mind to use my influence to have the whole thing taken away from here and set up in the North, where it would be a great convenience for travelling rabbits."

"You'd have to shift the cement works too," the practical Brownie reminded him.

But the Rabbit sat lost in wonder, gazing up at the lines of little buckets rocking gently on their cable, moving gradually in a long line as far as the eye could see. Then suddenly he started off down towards the cement works in the distance.

"Wait! Wait!" cried Brownie anxiously, racing after him. "Rabbit, listen to me. You don't know what you're doing. You'll be caught in a cement-mixer and ground in pieces, and what'll I say to your wife?"

The Rabbit stopped and looked at him witheringly. "I do not intend," he said, in dignified tones, "to travel down to the cement works on a heap of jagged stones and end up in a cement-mixer. I've more sense than that. I shall jump into an empty bucket going back to the quarry once I find a convenient place to get on. You'd better stay here, Brownie, since you're obviously scared. Watch out, and you'll see me passing."

So Brownie and his family waited, and after what seemed a very long time they could distinguish coming towards them one bucket which was not empty but had a head and two long ears sticking up over the side.

"Hurrah! Hurrah!" squeaked Brownie's excited children, jumping up and down with delight as the Rabbit sailed past, waving his paw and looking very pleased with himself. "Let's all go for a bucket ride, Daddy!"

"We'll wait and see what happens to him first," replied Brownie grimly.

The Rabbit in the bucket looked all round him, savouring every glorious moment of his ride. I've always wanted to fly, he said to himself, and this is nearly as good—gliding along over the countryside and feeling like a king!

Because the Rabbit felt like a king he began to act like one, and when he spied Ruairi Fox in a field far below him he gave a languid, condescending motion of the paw and bowed very haughtily in a manner calculated to madden the Fox. Next moment a clod of earth hit the bucket with a resounding *ping*, and the Rabbit shot six inches into the air and landed back in the rocking bucket the wrong way up. Of course, it was his own fault; he shouldn't have taunted the short-tempered Fox.

All went well for a little while after that: the Rabbit in his aerial carriage glided along over fields and roads and bridges, across little rivers and lanes, past thatched cottages and trees and gardens; he saw the cows going home to be milked, and the hens dashing wildly across the farmyard to where grain was being scattered, and a baker's van like a bright red bead threading its way along the road back to Drogheda. There they were, all struggling and striving and expending their energy; and here was he, Rabbit, being carried along effortlessly, sitting at his ease and looking down on the whole lot of them! Life was very pleasant for a clever Rabbit who knew how to make the most of it.

And just as the Rabbit was indulging in these pleasant thoughts the buckets stopped moving. At first he was not particularly worried, but after a few minutes he began to wonder what had gone wrong, and when he poked his head over the side to have a look the first thing he saw was Ruairi Fox on his back in a field, roaring with laughter.

"Ha, ha, ha, you silly Rabbit!" he crowed. "I suppose you never thought the buckets would stop when the day's work was done? You do look silly cocked up there! How are you going to get down?"

But the Rabbit only wished he knew himself how he was going to get down.

The bucket in which he sat had stopped just over a narrow country road bordered with hawthorn-hedges. Now and again some one on a bicycle would pedal by, and Ruairi would lie still under the hedge and the Rabbit crouch down in his bucket until the danger was past. Brownie and his family had by this time arrived in a hayfield on the other side of the road and were wringing their paws in dismay at the Rabbit's plight.

"I should never have let you go!" wailed Brownie. "I forgot to tell you that the cement works would be closing for the week-end. You'll have to stay there till Monday!"

*After a few minutes he began to wonder what
had gone wrong*

The Fox shrieked with laughter, Brownie and his family wept, and the Rabbit stayed in the bottom of the bucket out of sight just long enough to pull himself together and determine to put a brave face on his troubles. Then up he popped again, as bold as brass.

"Don't worry, Brownie," he called. "I'll get down somehow. See if you can find my friend the seagull anywhere about, and send him along."

Brownie's family sped off in every direction to look for the seagull, and soon one of the little bunnies discovered him fishing in the Boyne. He came at once to

the Rabbit's summons and perched on the overhead cable
to talk to him.

"Come down beside me," said the Rabbit. "I don't
want any passer-by to know I'm here."

"Right!" said the seagull. "Hold tight!"

With a plonk and a scrabbling of feet he landed in the
bucket, which swayed so violently that the Rabbit was
nearly pitched out for the second time, while down
below Brownie and his children clutched one another in
terror, and even Ruairi Fox blinked.

"If I climbed on your back could you fly me to the
ground?" the Rabbit asked the seagull.

The seagull shook his head. "I'm afraid it would be
a crash-landing," he said. "But I tell you what, Rabbit
—I'll scout around to see if there's a bus or cart or lorry
likely to be coming along this road; I'll give you due
warning, and you can be ready to jump down as it passes
underneath. It's not a big drop if you're careful."

"Oh, dear," said the Rabbit, "I could never leap on to
a moving bus. I'd fall off and land underneath it for sure."

"Then we must find some one who can stop the bus,"
said the seagull. "It will have to be an animal, though—
they never halt for a bird."

"Don't send Brownie," said the Rabbit anxiously.
"They'd just run over him."

"Or Ruairi," observed the seagull. "They'd knock
him down twice as fast. No, we want a bigger, more
noticeable animal. . . . I have it! There's Pansy Pony in
the field with the Fox; she knows how to lift the latch
of the gate with her nose and come out on to the road.
I'm sure she'd do what we want."

So off flew the seagull to ask Pansy for her help.

As he had thought, Pansy was only too delighted to
oblige. She was a good-natured little creature, but a

trifle vain, and there was nothing she liked better than to draw admiring glances as she pranced up and down, showing off her pretty figure with her glossy chestnut mane and long tail that nearly touched the ground. She came over at once to the gate and began to nose it open in readiness for her next public appearance.

Meanwhile the seagull had lighted again on the cable. "Pansy says there are no buses on this road," he informed the Rabbit, "but carts and lorries often pass by. I'm going to look for one now."

"Make it a hay-cart if you can," the Rabbit chipped in.

"Ach, you always want to travel first-class!" retorted the seagull, flying away.

Soon he was back with the news that a lorry laden with sacks of potatoes was in sight, making for the harbour. A thrill of excitement ran through the little company: the seagull sat on the cable ready to call out directions; the Rabbit stood poised with one leg over the edge of the bucket; Pansy was out at the gate; while through the hedge on one side of the road watched Ruairi Fox, and through the hedge on the opposite side peered a row of little bunnies, with Brownie in the middle. All the time the lorry could be heard coming nearer and nearer.

"Now, Pansy!" called the seagull from his vantage-point, and Pansy trotted into the middle of the road just as the lorry snored round the bend.

"*Honk, honk, honk!*" cried the lorry.

Pansy stood and looked at it with wide, wondering eyes. She was a good actress.

The lorry snarled into bottom gear in an effort to pass her.

"*Honk, honk, honk!*" it shouted, coming closer.

Then Pansy put on her prize performance. With terrified eyes and wild, tossing mane she reared and plunged and kicked, and pranced and danced and curvetted, and did everything short of turning a somersault.

The lorry braked, then drew to a standstill; indeed, there was nothing else it could do, for Pansy was taking up the whole road. "That beast must be away in the head," the lorry-driver remarked to his mate. "Will you get out or shall I?"

"You," said his mate.

"Jump, Rabbit!" screamed the seagull.

The Rabbit took a deep breath and jumped. "Ugh!" he groaned, landing on the hard, knobbly potatoes.

"That'll do, Pansy," directed the seagull, and just as the lorry-driver was preparing to clamber down from his cab Pansy suddenly quietened and came trotting past him with a mischievous little grin on her face.

"Maybe a wasp stung her," said the lorry-driver's mate.

"Ah, 'twas the flies most likely," remarked the driver, as he set the lorry into motion again. "The flies do be terrible bothersome to them in the heat."

Scrambling down over the sacks of potatoes, the Rabbit had managed to catch hold of Pansy's mane and climb on to her back just as the lorry started off with a jerk.

"Safe again, folks!" he cried gleefully.

"Ee-ee-ee! You're pulling my hair," Pansy complained.

"Sorry," said the Rabbit, "but I didn't want to fall off."

"You won't fall off if you settle yourself securely and rest your front paws lightly on either side of my neck," Pansy instructed him. "That's better. Shall I take you for a ride round my field?"

"Oh, yes, please!" said the Rabbit.

Pansy trotted through the opening, pausing to close the gate carefully behind her; then they made the circuit of the field, with the Rabbit bobbing up and down on her back, enjoying himself immensely. (Being a rabbit, he was used to travelling bobbity-bob, and liked the sensation.) "Look," he said, leaning forward to whisper in Pansy's ear, "there's Ruairi Fox skulking in under the hedge—chase him! Go on, for fun, let's chase him!" The lively Pony needed no second bidding for a romp, so with a great pounding of hoofs she startled the Fox out of his hiding-place and chased him round and round the field, urged on by jubilant whoops from the Rabbit, until at last Ruairi escaped through a hole in the hedge and bared his teeth at them from the other side.

"Ah, well," sighed the Rabbit regretfully, as he slid from Pansy's back to the ground, "and now the excitement's all over I suppose it must be nearly time for me to go home."

"Surely you're not thinking of leaving us already!" exclaimed Brownie, though secretly he was rather relieved at the prospect of getting rid of such an adventurous relation who kept him in a perpetual state of alarm.

"I'll be back soon," the Rabbit promised him, as he went round to bid good-bye to everybody, starting with Pansy. "Back for another ride in one of those delightful little buckets of yours."

"Do you mean to say you'd risk your life going up in one of those things again?" gasped Brownie. "Especially after all the trouble we've had in getting you down?"

"Next time there won't be any need to rescue me," the Rabbit assured him. "I've thought of a way to improve my technique. I'll find an old umbrella to use as a parachute, so that I can float down to the ground whenever I choose."

"That's the spirit!" said the seagull approvingly.

"You must be crazy!" muttered Brownie.

"Thank you for a wonderful holiday, Brownie," said the Rabbit, vigorously shaking his cousin's paw. "I'll be able to tell my wife when I go home about all I saw here, and how I rode bareback on a pony, and travelled overland on a cable railway—why, she'll be thinking I was away in Switzerland!"

The seagull chuckled.

The Rabbit turned to Brownie's good little children standing in a row, waiting to say good-bye. Patting their furry heads, he whispered, "Next time I come I'll bring your cousin Bobtail with me."

"Oh, goody, goody!" shrieked the little bunnies, jumping for joy.

With a last cheery wave the Rabbit scudded away into the gathering twilight, and all the others watched him out of sight. Soon even the seagull could see him no longer.

"Bed, bunnies!" called Brownie.

"Yes, Dad," replied the children, obediently falling into line behind him, ready to scamper home.

The seagull laughed again.

"What's the matter?" asked Brownie, pausing to glance up at him.

"Oh, nothing, nothing," said the seagull. "I was merely reflecting what an exciting time you're all in for when the Rabbit brings his son to visit you."

"Oh, dear!" sighed Brownie. "More trouble in store?"

"But definitely," chuckled the seagull, spreading his wings for flight. "Just wait till you meet Bobtail!"

H

8

When the Goat spoke Irish

~~~~~~

Once upon a time the Gaelic League held a meeting just under the hill where the Goat lived. The Goat listened to every impassioned word the speakers uttered in praise of the old tongue, and when they departed they left behind them at least one convert, for Puck had made up his mind henceforth to speak no language other than Irish. True, his Irish had grown a little rusty from lack of use, but that did not daunt him in the least.

"*Sláinte!*" he cried to the Rabbit speeding below through the glen.

The Rabbit sat back on his heels and pricked up his ears.

"What—did—you—say?" he called.

"*Sláinte!*" the Goat repeated. "*Sláinte!*"

Cupping his paws round his mouth, the Rabbit shouted louder, "CAN'T—HEAR—YOU!"

Without another word the Goat turned away and began to crop the turf.

Very well, said the Rabbit to himself, shrugging his shoulders, don't tell me; I don't care. And, dismissing the incident from his mind, he went about his business.

Next day he was unexpectedly reminded of it when, hearing a strange song come from behind a hedge, he popped through to find Agnes the Sheep on the other side, crooning a Gaelic lullaby to her little lamb.

"What's that you're singing, Agnes?" the Rabbit inquired brightly.

"It's a song my mother used to sing to us when we were lambs," said Agnes, "and her mother sang it to her. A traditional air, in fact. I'd nearly forgotten the words of it, but it's odd how the Irish comes back to you once you begin to use it again."

With that the Cow came along, and the Sheep greeted her in Irish and was answered in the same language.

The Rabbit (who was not an Irish-speaker himself) began to grow quite annoyed. "What's the meaning of this sudden flow of Irish in the district?" he said sharply. "Yesterday the Goat shouted something at me that I didn't understand. I'd be glad to know what it was. It sounded like 'shlunty.'"

"Oh, that's easy!" replied the Cow and the Sheep together. "It just means 'Your very good health.' It's a form of greeting, you know."

"Then why couldn't he say it in plain English?" grumbled the Rabbit.

The Cow spoke dreamily, as though she were repeating a lesson she had learnt. "Until a hundred years ago there was nothing but Irish spoken in these glens," she said.

"So what?" demanded the Rabbit, somewhat rudely. "We can't go back a hundred years!"

"If we lose our language we lose our culture, heritage, and our claim to nationhood," said the Sheep, with the same faraway look in her eyes.

"Nonsense!" retorted the Rabbit. "I'm as Irish as any of you, and I don't speak a word of the language."

"On what, then, do you base your claim to Irish nationality, Coney Rabbit?" sneered the Fox, who had sauntered up, drawn by the sound of voices.

"I was born here, I live here, and I love Ireland," replied the Rabbit. "What more could I need to be an Irish rabbit?"

"The language!" chorused the other three animals.

Then the Rabbit uttered something that is better not repeated in any language, and went home to his burrow.

"Is Bobtail about?" he asked his wife.

"I saw him a minute ago up among the whin-bushes on the hillside with his friends," said she. "They were playing 'Here are the rabbits coming through'—a nice, quiet game. What has he done?"

"Oh, nothing this time," the Rabbit assured her. "I just want him, that's all."

So off he went up the hillside and called Bobtail.

"Tell me, son," said the Rabbit confidentially, when the little bunny was at his side, "in that school you go to have they any Irish grammars or phrase-books?"

"Oh, yep, Pop!" cried Bobtail, in the nasal drawl he liked to affect. "Sure! Oodles of 'em. D'ya want one?"

"I'd like to—er—polish up my Irish if you could get me the loan of a book for a couple of weeks," said the Rabbit. "Ask the teacher."

"No fear!" returned Bobtail, with an expansive wink. "She might only scream, 'What's that rabbit doin' there?' I know the cupboard they're kept in, and I'll just pinch one. Leave it to me, Pop!"

And he dashed back to rejoin his friends, shouting at the top of his voice, "Stand and deliver! This is Bobtail, the highway-rabbit—your lettuce or your life!"

The Rabbit's eldest son Bobtail was a lively, curious youngster, who bade fair to become as fond of foreign expeditions as his father was. He had lately taken to frequenting Knocknacarry school, where he would steal in and sit behind the back row of children, not making a sound but listening intently to all that was said. Bobtail's ruling ambition was to get to know as much as his father—so his mother told him he couldn't start too soon!

Next day, sure enough, the little bunny brought home from school a tattered, dog-eared manual of Irish conversation. "Hey, Pop!" he called, slinging it into the mouth of the burrow as he sped past.

The Rabbit picked it up distastefully, wrinkling his nose. "He might have chosen a clean one," he grumbled.

"I'm sure he did his best, dear," said Bobtail's mother. "I expect they have the clean ones counted."

Great was Bobtail's amusement that night to observe his father muttering to himself as he conned Irish phrases out of the ragged book.

"Look at Pop doin' his homework!" chuckled Bobtail, pinching his little sister Fancy to make her squeak.

"Now, now, children," Katie Rabbit reproved them, "be good. Your father's very busy."

But they made so much noise that she had to put them to bed. She came back looking quite flustered, for Bobtail's voice could be heard shouting in the distance, "It's a shame, so it is! I didn't do nuthin'. Me an' Fancy, we're not stuffed rabbits—we wanna bit o' fun."

"Wouldn't you like to learn another language, Katie?" said the Rabbit, seeking a companion in his toil.

"No, thank you, dear," answered the Rabbit's wife. "It doesn't seem to me worth while, learning two ways of saying the same thing."

The Rabbit frowned at her and went on with his task. After an hour or so Katie Rabbit noticed her husband flicking over the pages to see how many were still left, and she smiled to herself. At last the Rabbit put down the book and sighed.

"This is more difficult than I expected," he said.

"I don't know why you bother, dear," remarked his wife, rising to get the supper. "I'm sure you know enough already."

"What?" exclaimed the Rabbit indignantly. "Let myself be worsted by a Goat? Not likely!" And he set to work again with more determination than ever.

One animal who sympathized with the Rabbit was Jess, the Sheepdog. She was a rough-haired Collie with a brindled shaggy coat and bright eyes that gleamed out under a fringe of hair, and, having been brought over from Yorkshire when she was a pup, she did not speak Irish either. "It wouldn't pay me to be a native speaker," Jess confided to the Rabbit. "Why, I'd lose all my foreign connexions!" And in proof of her claim Jess could point to a line of silver cups that adorned the sitting-room mantelpiece, trophies she had brought home from sheep-trials all over the country and even from places as far afield as Cumberland, Derby, and Galashiels. Since she spent so much of her time with her master, Jess cared little what language the other animals chose to speak; but, for friendship's sake, she declared herself willing to hold the book and hear the Rabbit repeat his lessons. She proved an invaluable aid, too, for the very first thing Jess did was to borrow a blue pencil from Bobtail and score out all the sentences that didn't apply to animals.

" 'I broke the chain of my bicycle as I was cycling to Tuam,' " she read. "You'll hardly want that one, Rabbit!" And out it went with a flourish of the blue pencil. " 'I left my trousers in press to put a crease in them,' " she read next, and that went out too. " 'Only for the tobacco I would never work,' " chuckled Jess, scoring vigorously.

"Excuse me, Jess," put in the Rabbit, his forehead puckered in dismay, "but please be more careful. That's a borrowed book."

"Oh, it's quite all right," said Jess airily. "I'm just editing it. All the very best firms keep an editor to score things out."

The Rabbit looked on with some misgiving, but Jess was clearly enjoying herself. When she presented him with the book again he found that she had left intact the greetings at the beginning and the proverbs at the end, but very little in between.

"Learn the greetings first," she advised him; and the Rabbit did so. As soon as he had mastered a few of the conventional Irish modes of address he sallied forth to try issues with the Goat.

"The blessing of St Patrick be upon you!" said the Goat in Irish (as the Rabbit knew he would).

"And the favour of St Brigid with yourself," responded the Rabbit piously.

For a moment Puck looked surprised, then he added, " May you have the blessed St Columcille to guide your steps this day!"

"And yourself the blessed St Kevin to make your bed this night," the Rabbit promptly replied.

Then the Goat was in a difficulty, for he could not think of any more Irish saints quickly enough. Besides, he was still turning over in his thoughts the last remark the Rabbit had made; and, recollecting the perilous kind of bed St Kevin had chosen for himself on a rocky ledge overhanging the dark waters of Glendalough, the Goat was wondering if it was a good wish or an ill wish the Rabbit had in mind for him. While he was considering the question the Rabbit suddenly called out, "One for me, Puck!" and scampered off. The Goat shouted something after him and, seeing the Cow smile, the Rabbit paused under her feet and whispered, "Maida! What did he say?"

The Cow paused to shift the wad of grass she was chewing into the other cheek. "He says it's one for him," she interpreted, "because you wouldn't be learning the Irish at all if it wasn't for his influence."

"What nonsense he talks!" said the Rabbit indignantly. "Why, I've quite a flair for the language, so I have!"

Encouraged by his moderate success, the Rabbit hurried home and buckled to with a will, memorizing the Irish sayings at the end of his book.

"Learn only the animal proverbs," Jess told him. "You'll never have occasion for any of the others." She was a great Dog for short cuts.

"All right," said the Rabbit, and he rhymed away to himself, " 'To every cow belongs her calf.' 'Don't give cherries to pigs.' 'Every bird as it is reared and the lark to the bog.' '"Isn't it I raised the dust!" said the fly behind the coach.' "

Jess half closed her eyes, for the Rabbit's repetition was making her feel sleepy.

"Here's a good one, Jess," he rattled on, absorbed in his discoveries. " 'If you put a silk dress on a goat it is still a goat!' And here's another I'll be able to work into my conversation: 'You will not have sense while there's snipe in a bog or a nose on a cat.' Oh, won't I love trying these out on Puck! But surely this is a queer one: 'One beetle knows another beetle.' Why beetles, I wonder? Why not horses or dogs or rabbits? Still, that's what it says in the book—'One beetle knows another beetle.' "

He looked up. "Are you listening, Jess? What does it mean?"

"It's an insult," answered Jess, with conviction. "Irish proverbs always turn out to be insults in disguise."

Before the Rabbit could reply a shrill whistle sounded from the direction of the farmhouse, and Jess sprang to her feet and raced away. She was a good Dog, whose master never needed to whistle her twice.

As the Rabbit did not see Jess during the next few days, he concluded that she must have gone on her travels again. Occasionally, to divert himself, he would waylay the Goat and provoke a short conversation in Irish with him, the animal who managed to get the last word in being accounted the winner. It was usually the Goat who won.

Then about a week later, when down in his burrow, the Rabbit heard a familiar bark, and, rushing up to the surface, he made for the farm. Jess was waiting at the gate for him, beaming with joy and brimful of excitement.

"Hallo, Rabbit!" she called. "How goes the Irish? You couldn't guess what thrilling news I have for you, you really couldn't!"

"You've been across the water and won another cup?" the Rabbit suggested.

"Ach, yes," said Jess, "but I wouldn't have called you specially to tell you that. It's easy enough for a dog to win at the sheep-trials if he knows how to go about it. It's all a question of studying the temperament of the sheep. Now, this last lot I had to deal with were wild, mountainy creatures brought down from the Cheviots, and I could see at a glance the mistake the other dogs were making in going too close to chivy the sheep and scaring the woolly wits out of them; so when my turn came I crawled flat through the grass, with my eyes fixed on them, moving by inches and always keeping my distance until I had the sheep just where I wanted them. Remote control, you know!"

"You're a very clever Dog, Jess," said the Rabbit admiringly.

"Oh, that's nothing!" Jess smiled. "If I couldn't do my job properly I wouldn't be much use in the world, would I? But what I meant to tell you is that after the sheep-trials were over my master and I went to a big fair—in the town of Berwick, I think it was; and could you guess what we bought there?"

"I could not," said the Rabbit, "but please don't keep me in suspense any longer, Jess. Tell me."

"Well, we got the loveliest, daintiest little Nanny-goat you've ever seen! Pure silvery white from tip to toe she is, with a coat as fine as silk and beautiful amber eyes, and the gait of a princess. She's well-connected, too—my master has her family tree all written down on a piece of paper in his breast-pocket. But oh, Rabbit, this is the best thing of all about her"—Jess was chuckling so much that she could hardly finish her sentence—"she doesn't know one single, solitary word of Irish! I'd like to see Puck's face when he meets her—he'll be in a queer predicament then!"

"Perhaps she'll be too grand to speak to our Goat," said the Rabbit hopefully.

"Oh, Puck has a pedigree himself," said Jess, "though indeed his manners don't match it. But this will test his fetish for the Irish tongue, mark my words! When I give a double bark repeated that will be a signal to you, Rabbit, to come and watch the fun—so be ready."

That same evening the little new Goat arrived by transport lorry, and the children fussed round her and caressed her and named her Pearlie. When she had had a few days to accustom herself to her fresh surroundings her master took her up the hill to introduce her to Puck. With him went his small son, and following at their heels came Jess, uttering a series of short double barks. As soon as they had reached the field Jess retired to the hedge, to watch the proceedings from there.

"Where's the Dog?" asked her master, looking round.

"She's over there by the ditch, talking to that Rabbit," piped the little boy. He pointed in their direction.

The man showed no trace of surprise, having realized long ago that he owned an exceptionally intelligent Dog who would much rather talk to a rabbit than chase one.

When first he had heard the barks of the approaching Dog and the voice of his master drawing nearer Puck had resolutely turned his back upon the gate by which they must enter. They were English-speakers, both of them; he would have no truck with them. Feigning to be quite unconscious of their presence in the field, the Goat tugged away at the hedge where the leaves were young and green. Then, all of a sudden, he heard a sound that he could not ignore, a plaintive, feminine note of appeal that was something between a bleat and a cry. He swung round to face the oncomers, and his eyes rested on the radiant, sylph-like figure of little Pearlie. A wave of awestruck admiration crossed the Goat's face, for never had he visualized a creature so beautiful as this, who seemed to him an angel strayed from some unknown caprine heaven.

"May St Patrick's blessing go with you!" he said, in a voice full of feeling.

At the unfamiliar tongue the little Nanny-goat drew back a step.

"And St Brigid be guarding your footsteps," he added, advancing.

She retreated still farther, until she stood poised on a tussock of grass, ready at any moment to take her flight to the far end of the field.

"You're very beautiful," said the Goat huskily, and he called her '*a mhuirnín*,' which (as even the Rabbit knew) means 'darling.'

Responding to his tone, if not his words, Pearlie managed to falter, "I'm sorry, sir. I'm afraid I don't understand your language."

Puck was seen to swallow hard; for a few seconds principle waged war with inclination; then he found his voice and answered—in English—"That's all right, my dear. I'll speak any language you wish."

An expression of incredulous delight swept over Pearlie's face, and she straightway tripped over to him and began to chatter as friendly as you like.

Jess, in the hedge, missed nothing of this. She gave the Rabbit a nudge, and they both began to giggle.

"Come on," said the farmer to his son. "We've work to do. Pearlie will be all right with Puck," he added, seeing that the boy was disposed to linger. "We'll leave them to make friends."

"Oh, isn't it splendid?" cried the Rabbit, hugging himself in sheer joy. "No more Irish verbs for me to learn, no more vocabularies, no more homework! I can get Bobtail to take the old book back to the school any time. I feel like shouting 'Hurrah,' Jess!"

"Don't be too sure," said the Dog, with a teasing glint in her eye. "Even if the Goat does go back to talking English, what about the others?"

"Oh, the rest don't matter," the Rabbit asserted confidently. "It was only Puck who kept them at it. Mind you, it isn't that I don't admire a good linguist," he continued (since he always tried to be perfectly fair), "but what I couldn't stand was the way Puck rammed the Irish down my throat at every opportunity."

"I quite agree," Jess responded. Their conversation was broken by a sudden sharp whistle; and up got Jess in a flurry. "Must go now. Sorry, Rabbit!" she muttered, and, squeezing out between the bars of the gate, she streaked down the hill after her master.

So it was left to the Rabbit to say the last word—and the Rabbit, believe it or not, said it in Irish! He had been watching Pearlie and Puck as they wandered slowly away together across the sunlit field; he was not slow to notice how the once arrogant Puck was gallantly showing his lady where the most savoury leaves and the aromatic herbs grew; and he smiled to himself as he murmured, "That's love!" A little imp of mischief danced in the Rabbit's face, and with paws up to his mouth he called after them as loudly as he could, "Hey, Puck! ONE —BEETLE —KNOWS —ANOTHER —BEETLE!" Then he darted away without waiting for a reply.

And was the Goat angered by the Rabbit's taunts? Why, Puck was so entranced that he neither heard nor heeded him; for love is stronger than language.

9

The Cat who went to Sea

~~~~~~

Who gave you nine lives, Pussy?" asked the Horse.

"The witch I used to work for, of course," replied the Cat, elegantly arching her neck to lick the fur along her spine.

"Then you really were a witch's Cat, no mistake?" the Horse said. "That time I fished you out of the sea and you shouted, 'My eighth life gone!' I thought you were only joking. Were you serious?"

"I was," said the Cat. "I'm down to my last life now, like the rest of you."

"My word, you must have been extravagant!" exclaimed the Horse. As the Cat merely shrugged her shoulders by way of reply he stopped teasing her and said, "Tell me about the witch. What was her name?"

"Old Biddy Brush," smiled the Cat reminiscently. "She was good to me, too, was Biddy. Took me everywhere with her on the broomstick and taught me all I know about the black art. But then when the time came that people all up and down the countryside were burning witches old Biddy says to me, says she, 'Grimalkin' (that was her spell-name for me), 'Grimalkin, I'm away to darkest Africa in the morning—is there anything I can do for you before I go?'"

"Why didn't you go with her?" interrupted the Horse.

"For the very good reason that I wasn't asked," replied the Cat. "Anyway, the middle of Africa, where she was bound for, is full of cats far bigger and fiercer than me, and what sort of a life would I have had mixed up with the likes of them? When Biddy asked me what I wanted I didn't know how to answer, so says I, 'Thank you kindly, mem, but I'll leave it to yourself'; and with that she began to weave a spell over me, tapping me every so often on the head with her bony forefinger, and this (so far as I can remember) is what she chanted:

> "'Claws that scratch and teeth that bite,
> Eyes that find the way by night,
> Legs that leap and feet that flee—
> Safe, Grimalkin, may you be.
> With skill to hunt and wit to steal
> No pangs of hunger may you feel;
> This my gift to you I give—
> The space of nine lives you shall live.'

"Then she made me spin round nine times with my tail in my mouth while she said the last words of the enchantment:

"'Safe by land and safe by sea,
Grimalkin, you shall ever be.
By wind and rain and moon and sun
Safe till nine cats' lives have run.
Peace! Be still! The spell is done.'

"With that she disappeared up the chimney in a cloud of smoke, and I never glimpsed hilt nor hair of her again, not from that day to this."

"Wasn't that wonderful!" sighed the Horse. No witch had ever taken a personal interest in him, and he felt the Cat to have been highly privileged. Perhaps, he reflected, that was what gave Puss such haughty airs— the knowledge that she had once been a witch's familiar. Indeed, she was about to sail off, considering the conversation finished, when the Horse called her back.

"Puss," he said, "don't go away without telling me some more. However did you manage to run through eight lives at such a rate? What were you doing?"

"I couldn't begin to tell you eight life-stories, Bob!" the Cat protested. "Sure, we'd be here all night."

"Just one or two, then," said the Horse persuasively, smoothing out a place for her to sit in the grass beside him. "I'm a home-loving animal myself, but I do like to hear about other people's adventures—then I can think about them when I'm doing some humdrum task like pulling the plough, and I find I'm at the end of the furrow far more quickly."

"Oh, well," said the Cat, "one doesn't have to be very daring or adventurous to lose a life, you know. The first time it happened to me was when I was still a kitten and had climbed to the top of a high tree and couldn't get down again. I squalled for help, you may be sure, but nobody came, and in the end I had to jump. I landed on my feet all right—cats do—but with such a shock that I felt as if something had exploded inside my head, and I said to myself, That's my first life gone! If there had only been an older cat there to tell me to turn round and clamber down backward I'd have managed it without difficulty, but I didn't know the secret at the time; and so that's how I wasted one life."

The Horse nodded sympathetically, encouraging the Cat to talk on.

"Another time," she continued, "I tried to squeeze through some railings that were too close together— and I stuck! I really thought it was the end of me that time; there was such a hue and cry, and a crowd of people all gathered round to give me their advice, though a lot of good that was to me with my head caught between iron railings. In the end some one thought of fetching the strong man from the circus to bend the railings apart—half an inch did it—and set me free. That was another life gone (my fourth, I think it was), but ever since then I've known not to try to squeeze through where my whiskers won't fit. Whiskers don't go—Cat won't go. That's the lesson I learnt."

"Do you always learn a lesson when you lose a life?" the Horse asked.

"Of course," she replied. "There wouldn't be much point in throwing away a life and not learning *something*, would there?"

"I suppose not," said the Horse. "I never thought about it before. Tell me, Puss, and I won't ask you any more— what was the most exciting adventure you ever had?"

"I don't need to think twice about that," the Cat replied, with a smile. "It was the time I went to sea."

"You—went—to—sea?" repeated the Horse incredulously. "But I thought cats hated the water and never went near it if they could help it."

I

"We never go *into* it if we can avoid it," the Cat corrected him, "but there are lots of sea-going cats, Bob, cats who live on boats, cats who have made the Navy their profession and who'd be bored with a shore job—hundreds of 'em all over the world. However, I'm not one of that kind. You can bet your shoes and harness that when *I* went to sea it was a pure accident; nothing was farther from my thoughts. I was staying down in Portavogie at the time, where I had gone for the fishing-season, and one day as I was wandering across the beach near the harbour I came on an old fish-box. Now, there's nothing more delightful than the rich aroma of an ancient, salty, scaly box that has once held herrings——"

"Ugh!" muttered the Horse, with a grimace.

"—so after I had walked round it several times sniffing in the fragrance," the Cat continued, "I hopped on to the top of the box and looked inside to see if by any chance there might be some little fish left in it. There weren't, of course, but it was snug and comfortable inside the shallow box—much more comfortable for me than lying on the pebbly shore—so I settled down to bask in the sun. After a while, what with the heat of the July sun and my sense of well-being and content-ment, I must have fallen asleep, for the next thing I remember was feeling the box beneath me moving, swaying gently and rocking up and down. I lifted my head in alarm, and what I saw then filled me with terror, for the box in which I was lying had floated out to sea, and the shore was receding farther from me every moment! Soon I couldn't even sit down any more, for the water came seeping through between the boards till my vessel was awash, and when I stood up I was drenched with spray flying off the crests of the waves. Have you ever been to sea, Bob?"

"I have, to be sure," replied the Horse. "I crossed over from Portaferry to Strangford and back in a kind of landing-barge, that time I was entered for a ploughing-match near Downpatrick. There were two of us going over (the Savages' Horse, Jem, was with me) and truly it was a horrifying experience to feel the barge heaving under our feet and see the tide-race sliding past. Gave me quite a headache, it did. I couldn't see straight when I got off that barge, and Jem was staggering. No wonder we couldn't win any prizes that day! And then when we were brought back to Strangford quay at night and Jem got a glimpse of the waves beyond the harbour didn't he refuse to set hoof on the barge! Kicked up his heels and made such a shindy—his master was fair raging with him. But Jem got his way in the end, for they had to put him in a horse-box and take him the whole fifty miles round by road. Oh, I know how it feels to go to sea, Puss. I'd rather swim across any day!"

"There was no question of my swimming," said the Cat. "I was much too far out by that time. All I could do was cling on in desperation, digging my claws into the wood, while the raft went spinning dizzily up the side of one great wave and plunging into the trough of the next, with my stomach always floating down a split second after the rest of me. Sick and cold and terrified, I began to wonder what old Biddy Brush would have done in my place, and suddenly I remembered her as I had seen her once standing up in the midst of a tempest with her rags whipped about her and calling on the Celtic gods to come to her aid. I thought I might as well have a try, too, so I opened my mouth and screamed with all my might for Manannán,[1] the god of the sea, to look down upon me and bring me safe to shore."

[1] This is the god after whom the Isle of Man was named.

"Wasn't it well you knew to do that?" said the Horse admiringly. "It's a great thing, is education. And so you were rescued by Manannán?"

"Ah, but it's not just so simple as that," Puss replied. "You see, Bob, there's a big disadvantage in having your wishes granted by one of the old Celtic gods: they can't send you an unmixed blessing, for they're a mixture of good and evil themselves, so even if they do grant you your request it won't be long till you find a catch in it somewhere."

"Oh, dear!" sighed the Horse. "Isn't life complicated? But he saved you, that's the main thing."

"He did," the Cat admitted grudgingly, "but where do you think he took me to? No less a place than his own island! Do you know anything about Manannán's island, Bob?"

"Can't say I do—except that it's away by itself in the middle of the Irish Sea. Isn't that the one? A friend of mine saw it on his way across from Liverpool."

"He didn't mention anything about the cats there?"

"Oh, no," said Bob. "I tell you he only saw it from the boat as he was passing. He noticed the lighthouse flashing and asked what it was. Why, what about the cats?"

"I'd better tell you the whole story," Puss replied. "After I had been buffeted by the winds and soused by the spray for hours and hours, and it was past midnight in the grey dark of a summer's night, I began to see lights glimmering off and on as I rose and fell with the waves, and I heard the sound that the water makes when it crashes on a rocky shore—but before I had time to gather my wits properly the box I was floating in struck a submerged rock, and I was somersaulted into the cold, wet sea. I coughed and spluttered as I splashed towards the shore, but fortunately I hadn't far to go, and soon I was scrambling on to dry land, feeling more dead than alive. I could see the lamps shining in the town beyond, but before I went a step farther I sat down to wash my fur and make myself presentable."

"I'd have thought you were wet enough already, Puss," said the Horse playfully.

"Salty-wet, that's horrible," the Cat shuddered. "Makes my fur all sticky and nasty. As soon as I was looking spruce again I set off for the town. It was very late by now, but I was pretty sure there'd be some cats still about, and I hoped to find one who'd give me board and lodging till I could find a way of getting home again. On I went, through deserted streets, and then at last I spied a little kitten and called out to her. She took one glance at me, shrieked with alarm, and disappeared down a side-alley as fast as she could sprint. Silly little thing! thought I; what's upset her? And I continued on my way. Two or three times I saw other cats and hailed them, but the moment they caught a glimpse of me they too scuttled away into the night. Luckily, one of them who had been gnawing a huge bone for his supper left it behind him in his haste, so I was able to relieve my hunger at long last. Soon the milkman came out on his rounds, and by dint of knocking down a bottle that he left on a doorstep I got something to drink, too. Then I found an outhouse with a pile of sacks thrown in a corner where I lay down and slept, and slept, and slept."

Bob yawned in sympathy. "I'm sure you needed that sleep, Pussy," he said. "And did you ever solve the mystery of the scared cats?"

"Wait till I tell you," Puss went on. "When I wakened the next night (I had slept right through the day) what should I see but a ring of faces round me—

whiskered, furry faces—and cats' eyes glowing in the dark! The whole outhouse was thronged with them. Every cat in the town must have been there—perhaps every cat on the island, for all I know. When I stood up and stretched myself they all shrank back, 'oooh-ing' and 'ah-ing' and spitting at me, but I ignored the silly creatures and made for the door. As soon as I was outside in the street their leader stopped me. He was a

" He was a large fat Cat"

large fat Cat whom the others addressed as Lord Tom. 'Just a minute, you,' he said. 'We want you to answer some questions.'

"'Certainly,' said I. 'What would you like to know?'

"'Sit down,' he grunted.

"I might have refused, but there were too many of them for me to try any tricks, and, besides, I had noticed by this time how battle-scarred and tough Lord Tom was, and I knew that in my condition, after the ordeal of a sea-voyage and a day's starvation, I'd be no match for a big bully like him. He must have met some right fighters in his day, I thought, for they had left him without any tail, not even a shred of tail!

"Lord Tom sat down, and beside him was his wife, whom he called Polly, and opposite them was myself, and in a ring all around were the other cats, listening.

" 'What's your name?' growled Lord Tom.

" 'Grimalkin,' said I.

" 'Not a good name,' said Polly.

" 'Where do you come from?' he asked next.

" 'Ireland,' said I.

" 'Not a good place,' said Polly.

" 'You shut up!' I told her. I wasn't going to have her, or any other stranger, insulting my homeland.

"You should have heard the uproar then! Lord Tom was furious because I had been rude to Polly, and Polly glowered at me with all the concentrated wickedness that a cat is capable of. He wanted her to go away but she wouldn't, not till she had seen what would become of me. There was a pause while various cats came up and spoke to him and went away again, and then with a shock I noticed what I should have seen long before— that not a single cat among them boasted a tail! I was flabbergasted. They couldn't all have been fighting. Was it some disease that had made their tails drop off? But even the little kittens had none. I understood now why the kitten had run away from me the previous night, and why the grown cats all stared at me so hard and 'oooh-ed' and 'ah-ed' every time I moved. Perhaps they were descended from hares or rabbits, I decided. Anyhow, it was all most peculiar.

" 'Silence!' bawled Lord Tom. 'You,' he said. 'You're an unwanted alien. How did you get here in the first place?'

" 'I was shipwrecked,' I answered.

" 'A likely story!' sneered Polly. 'Ask him to prove it.'

"Well, of course I couldn't prove it, for dear only knows where the fish-box was by that time, but I told them my story anyway, and I could see unbelief written on all their faces.

" 'We know what you are,' thundered Lord Tom, when I had finished. 'You're a spy!'

" 'Oh, don't be so absurd,' I said wearily, for I was growing tired of their farce by this time and I wanted peace to think out some means of getting back to my old home in Ireland.

" 'Of course you're a spy!' shrieked Polly, coming close to me and spitting in my face. 'What would you be doing with an aerial transmitter if you weren't a spy?'

" 'A what?' said I, astonished.

" 'An aerial transmitter,' she repeated, 'for sending wireless messages. Look at it, standing straight up and quivering!'

"And with one accord they all stretched out their paws and pointed accusingly to my tail!

" 'Why, that's my tail!' I sang out, laughing at their ignorance.

" 'Listen,' said Lord Tom solemnly. 'Dogs have tails to wag at their masters, and cows and horses have tails to swish at the flies, but what would a cat be doing with a tail? Answer me that.'

" 'But all cats——' I began, then I stopped short. What would be the use of my explaining that I had never seen cats without tails until I met them? They wouldn't believe me. Nevertheless, I had to say something. 'In Ireland, where I come from,' I said, 'every cat has a tail.'

" 'A likely story!' sniffed Polly. 'Can you prove it?'

" 'Yes,' said I. 'All you have to do is come to Ireland and see for yourself.'

" 'Look here,' Lord Tom rumbled in his throat, his fur beginning to rise, 'are you trying to entice my wife to run away with you?'

" 'That scraggy old thing?' I cried. 'Not likely! I wouldn't take her as a gift.'

"He nearly blew up with rage for the second time that night. His eyes shone, and I saw him gathering himself together for a mighty spring, but before he could reach me I upped and flew over the heads of the onlookers and streaked for the harbour. It had just come into my mind that the thing I must do was to find a ship that would take me out of there in double-quick time.

" 'After him!' shouted Lord Tom.

" 'Off with his tail!' bawled the others, and they all gave chase.

"I ran and ran, and before long I was aware that the pursuit was slackening. Lord Tom was too heavy to move fast, and the others had no heart for the chase. I think they were afraid of me, for every time I screeched they seemed to imagine that I was sending out radio messages for help, and so they dropped farther and farther behind, till soon they weren't in sight at all.

"I walked along the quayside and I looked in at every porthole and listened to the drifts of conversation that were floating out on the night air, while I made up my mind which ship I was going to board.

"By and by I approached one from which came a very tempting smell of cooking. I paused to sniff, and as I did so I heard one sailor say to another, 'Sammy, reach me thon baccy-box fornenst the wireless, like a good fella. Man, that fry was quare and tasty, but it woulda been better still with a farl o' soda bread fried in the pan along wi' it.'

" 'Never mind,' came the reply, 'the morrow's morn will see us passing the Copelands. . . .'

"Do you know, I could have stood on my hind legs and cheered when I heard them! A Belfast boat! I said to myself. They'll be steaming up Belfast Lough to-morrow! Oh, my fur and whiskers, this suits me! And before you could say 'Dick Whittington' I had sped up that gangway, across the deck, down the companion-way, and into the hold. There I found the ship's Cat, a friendly old soul who shared his supper with me. He was glad of company, as he didn't often have any in the normal way. He was highly amused when I told him how relieved I was to see that he had a tail: he had never thought much about tails before, but then neither had I until my adventure at sea. And so I reached Belfast, and walked back to my home in the Ards, none the worse except for the shock I had experienced and the life I had lost at sea."

"What a fascinating story!" said Bob the Horse, with a long sigh. "It's a wonderful tale."

"Do you really think so?" smiled the Cat. "I'm glad. I've always been rather proud of it, you know." She contemplated her long silky tail with the utmost satisfaction.

Bob and she didn't mean the same thing at all, but as they were both so pleased, I suppose that didn't matter.

10

The Night they talked of Ghosts

〰〰〰〰〰〰〰〰〰〰〰〰〰〰〰〰〰〰〰〰

If you had only been with me last night," said Curly, the Ram, "it would have made your fur and whiskers bristle!"

"Oh, what?" cried the animals.

"I was lying in the heather just above Loughareema," Curly continued, "when all of a sudden I heard the sound of horses' hooves and the jingle of harness and the hum of carriage-wheels along the road, and I wondered to myself who could be passing by so near to midnight—and the next moment there came a confused splashing sound and a terrible cry and then silence. I got up from among the crags, and I looked down on the lough shining in the moonlight, but there wasn't as much as a ripple on its surface. Then I knew it was the phantom coach I had heard."

"Colonel MacNeill's coach, that drove into the lough years and years ago?" the Horse asked.

"The very same," Curly nodded. "Two or three times before last night I thought I heard it, but I could never be certain that it wasn't just the wind, or my fancy."

"Didn't you *see* nuthin'?" came the shrill voice of a little bunny. "No headless horseman, nor nuthin'?"

The Ram shook his head. "Nothing."

"Is that you, Bobtail?" called the Rabbit. "It's past your bedtime. Off with you, now!"

"Aw, Pop!" groaned Bobtail. "Just when the stories are gettin' good!"

"Run along," the Rabbit insisted. "Ghost stories aren't for little bunnies. They'll only give you nightmares."

Bobtail sidled off sulkily and appeared to go away, but he didn't really go at all. He squatted down quietly behind the Cow where his father couldn't see him, and there he listened, all ears, to the rest of the ghost stories.

"Of course I often see strange things myself," the Horse was saying. "My family has always been psychic——"

"Is that why you shy at nothing in the road?" interrupted the Mule maliciously.

"On the contrary, we shy at *something* in the road." replied the Horse, with dignity, "only you're too dense to see it. Even human beings admit that we horses are especially sensitive to the supernatural. That's why you'll find more equine ghosts than all other animal ghosts put together."

This statement provoked loud, indignant cries from his hearers, who all had family ghosts to boast of, it seemed—all except the Rabbit. Though the Rabbit thought back earnestly through his long family history, he could not unearth a rabbity ghost anywhere. For some reason this annoyed him exceedingly. Meanwhile the Horse went on talking.

"It stands to sense," he said, "that when men started coming back as ghosts they'd bring their horses with them—couldn't do without them, in fact. Why, the great battles of Ireland have been fought over and over again with ghostly men and horses; and everybody knows that the ancient warriors of Ireland, the Fianna, who lie sleeping in a cavern in the hills, have their horses at their side——"

"And their hounds," put in the Dog.

"That's as may be," continued the Horse. "Their horses, anyway. As for ghostly horsemen, there are so many of those that I couldn't hope to name them all. Travelling people out early on a May morning have often seen the princely O'Donoghue gallop across the waters of Killarney on Crebough, his white charger. Then there's the bygone Earl of Kildare who sits encased in armour on his mighty war-steed and reviews his shadowy troops on the Curragh of Kildare. And Gerald, the Wizard Earl, I mustn't forget him. Every seventh year he comes out of the depths of Lough Gur and rides once round the lake before morning; this he must do, they say, until the silver shoes of his horse shall be worn as thin as a cat's ear. But need I tell you any more such tales? You yourselves must have heard the sounds of phantom horsemen go by from time to time on the road below."

"Indeed, indeed, we have," murmured the cows and sheep and goats.

"On All Souls' Night," said one old Sheep, shaking her head solemnly, "the road does be thronged with them."

"But how do you know they're ghosts?" put in the Rabbit. "They could be living men and horses. Did you go down and look?"

"There's not a doubt of it," the Sheep reaffirmed.

"No doubt at all," echoed the Cow.

"Because some of them are travelling by the old road where there is no road any more," the Horse concluded.

Though silenced, the Rabbit was not convinced. Having no ghost of his own, he had assumed a highly sceptical attitude to the whole discussion.

The Dog was the next speaker. "Many a one in

these parts," he said, "has heard Bran and Sceolaun, the hounds of Finn Mac Cumhaill, baying in the summer twilight. They are good, kindly dogs who would do nobody any harm. So is the little white faery dog that runs through the wood. But in the isle of the sea-god Manannán there's the phantom of the great black dog of Peel, who comes forth with eyes like burning coal and jaws dripping, and whoever meets him on the road has a right to be afraid, for the very sight of him means death."

The animals listened spellbound, giving an occasional shudder that was not altogether disagreeable.

"Tell me, Flick," the Rabbit whispered to the Hare, "have you any ghosts in your family?"

"Only me," said Flick. "I turn white in the winter-time." He screeched with laughter.

"You're a very silly animal," the Rabbit retorted, and left him.

The animal voices were tumbling in now, one after the other, each eager to tell of the ghosts he knew.

"The Gormanston foxes are famous," cried a sharp, yappy voice. "They cover the lawn of the big house when the old lord does be dying within."

"But surely those are *living* foxes," the Rabbit objected, "not ghostly ones at all."

"How do you know? You're not a fox," snapped Ruairi. "You've no right to express an opinion."

"I know when anybody's cheating," the Rabbit maintained.

"Cheating, am I?" snarled the Fox, edging closer. "Just you say that again, Coney Rabbit!"

"Oh, do stop quarrelling, you two," pleaded the Sheep, "or we'll have to break up the meeting. Keep away from him, Ruairi."

"There used to be a ghostly cat in Dublin"—next came a mewly tone—"a poor, unfortunate pussy-cat who chased a rat down in behind the organ-pipes in Christ Church and couldn't get out again. Her little ghost cried and cried for release down all the long years, but it wasn't set free till centuries afterwards when some workmen doing repairs opened the wall and found her skeleton along with that of the rat."

"She got her deserts, that one," murmured a grumpy Rat.

The Rabbit noticed that during these tales the Cow had been silently chewing the cud without offering to take part in the conversation, and he began to pluck up heart, thinking that she must be in the same position as himself with no ghosts to speak of. He padded across to where the Cow was lying, and, nudging her playfully, he whispered, "How about you, Maida? Any spooks in your family?"

She turned her large liquid eyes full upon him. "There are ghostly cows, of course," she answered, in her dreamy way. "Listen!" Then, closing her eyes, in a deep, poetic voice the Cow began to chant:

> "The murmur of the mourning ghost
> That keeps the shadowy kine,
> 'Oh, Keith of Ravelston,
> The sorrows of thy line!'"

It sounded very dramatic and effective, though apart from the "shadowy kine" it had not really very much to do with cows.

Now all this time Bobtail had been hiding behind the Cow's broad back, but once his father came so near he felt no longer safe, and while Maida was intoning her poetic piece he took the opportunity to steal away into

the bushes and make for home. As he went Bobtail had
an idea. Pop sure seems worried because we haven't
got a ghost in the family, he said to himself, and he gave
a very mischievous chuckle.

When the Cow had finished her recitation (which
lasted for ten more verses) and opened her eyes again
she found that the gathering of animals had already
begun to break up around her; this was unfortunately
rather apt to happen whenever the Cow recited. Having
said their good-nights, the animals went off in little
groups, parting reluctantly where their ways divided,
since they were all in a somewhat nervous state after
listening to so many eerie stories.

The Rabbit, lolloping off home on his own, had
almost reached his burrow when a white figure rose
abruptly from the path and confronted him.

"Wah! Wah!" it cried. "Woo! Woo!"

The Rabbit got such a shock that he jumped clean six
inches off the ground. Then his sharp ears detected a
snigger—yes, distinctly the ghost had sniggered! In a
flash the Rabbit sprang forward to grab the white
figure. Something writhed between his paws and was
gone—a small, brown body scudding away into the
darkness, showing still a bobbing gleam of white as it
sped—while the Rabbit was left foolishly clutching a
sheet of newspaper! He remembered now having
noticed that newspaper lying among the bracken earlier
in the day. Somebody had used it to give him a scare.
Why, Bobtail! Who else could it have been but Bobtail? The impudence of the little beggar! The Rabbit
strode back indignantly to his burrow.

He found his wife Katie sitting up for him, waiting in
a half-doze.

"Where's Bobtail?" he demanded.

"In bed, dear," Katie replied, blinking. "Ages ago. Why?"

"I saw him outside just now."

"Oh, you couldn't have," Katie assured him. "You must be mistaken."

"How can you tell where he is?" said the Rabbit rudely. "You were asleep."

"Indeed I wasn't," Katie denied emphatically. "Sure, I was waiting up for you! Well, I may have dropped off for a few moments, but I wasn't really asleep. I'd have heard anybody go out or come in. Oh, dear, now don't start wakening the little bunnies!"

She hurried anxiously after her husband as he pushed on into the part of the burrow where the family slept. Peering over his shoulder, she saw to her relief that they were all there, every one, and Bobtail among them, fast asleep.

"You see?" she said. "Now, come away, dear, don't disturb them."

The Rabbit stood frowning. "Next time I go out at night," he declared in a loud voice to no one in particular, "I shall go armed with a stout stick, just in case I should chance to meet any ghosts on the way."

"Ghosts, dear?" breathed Katie, her voice faint with alarm.

"That's what I said," the Rabbit reaffirmed. "Moreover, I'm warning any ghost who may happen to be listening that if I catch him at such silly pranks again he won't be able to sit down for a week." Catching Katie's eye, he added gruffly, "There's such a thing as respect, you know."

Katie shook her head in uneasy bewilderment. As for Bobtail, the only answer that came from him was a deep, heavy snore!

K

11

How the Rat kept Goal

〜〜〜〜〜〜〜〜〜〜〜〜〜〜〜〜〜〜〜〜〜

Whiskers the Rat was lying in the long grass by the side of the path, thoughtfully gnawing a root, when suddenly there bounced past his nose something that looked like a bright-red berry. Instinctively Whiskers darted out and caught it.

"Hey!" came an indignant shout from a leprechaun running down the hill. "Leave that alone. That's our ball."

"Here you are," said Whiskers, politely handing it over to the hot and breathless little gentleman, "but I saved you a journey to the foot of the hill, you know."

Without a word of thanks the leprechaun grabbed the ball and sped off with it, and Whiskers carried on with his own affairs.

He had completely forgotten the episode when later that evening a knock on the stone at the entrance of his

hole made him peep out, to find there a little company
of leprechauns, including the one he had already met.
Their leader was a dignified little old man with a white
beard, who carried the red ball under his arm.

"Excuse me, sir," he said to Whiskers, "I was wondering if we could sign you on for our Gaelic football
team, the Blessington Beagles?"

"Dear me, and I thought leprechauns always played
hurley!" Whiskers remarked.

"I suppose leprechauns can play whatever game they
like?" retorted the little man rather testily, then, getting a nudge from his neighbour, he continued in a more
even tone. "As I was about to say, in a week's time we
have to meet our old rivals from the County Kildare—
the Punchestown Warriors—and our object is to field
the strongest possible combination of talent in an effort
to retrieve our previous defeats."

"You mean you're going all-out to win?" said the
Rat, who liked plain speaking.

"Exactly," replied the leprechaun. "I'm the manager
of this team, and on the recommendation of our captain
here I'm willing to try you out in goal. He tells me you
can catch the ball miraculously; if we could only have
you on our side next Saturday we should knock those
Punchestown leprechauns spinning off the field. Will
you come?"

"I'm afraid I wouldn't be eligible," said Whiskers,
coming all the way out of his hole. "I'm not a leprechaun, you see; I'm a Rat."

The leader of the leprechauns gave a little cough.
"We realize that," he admitted, "but our plan was to
lend you a pair of breeches to cover your tail. Once your
tail is hidden nobody will ever notice that the chap in
goal is not a leprechaun."

"Do you think that would be quite fair?" asked Whiskers dubiously.

"There's nothing whatever in the rules against it," declared the little man irritably. "In my book of rules it says that a team shall consist of fifteen players. *Players*, mark you—it doesn't say they all have to be leprechauns. I can show it to you if you don't believe me."

"Oh, it's quite all right," Whiskers reassured him. "I'll take your word for it, though I'm afraid it *means* leprechauns, all the same."

"We wouldn't resort to such unprofessional tactics," the leprechaun captain explained, "except out of sheer desperation. The Punchestown Warriors have beaten us five times in succession, and we feel that not only our reputation but the honour of the whole County Wicklow is at stake."

"You can count on me, in that case," Whiskers promised him. "Show me what to do, and I'll try my best for the honour of Wicklow."

"By the way, it's against the rules to play any foreign game so long as you're a member of our club," the manager told Whiskers, before the leprechauns went away. "If you're found taking part in one you'll be suspended. Do you play soccer, rugger, or any other foreign game?" he demanded, as the Rat was looking doubtful.

"I sometimes have a round of tiddlywinks with the Rat next door," Whiskers confessed.

"Bah! That wasn't what I meant at all!" snapped the little man, and he stalked off in a temper, muttering something about common rodents, which Whiskers thought very unfair in the circumstances.

For the whole of the next week the Rat went into training for the big match. The leprechauns stuck to their original intention of placing him in goal; Whiskers was too bulky and not nimble enough for the forward line, but he made a splendid goalkeeper. He stood between two boulders while the leprechauns kicked the ball at him from every direction, and Whiskers was nearly always able to stop it. Unfortunately, he did not do quite so well when he had to wear breeches; he was so used to balancing with the help of his long tail that he took several tumbles before he could grow accustomed to having it curled up in a bundle behind him; however, both he and the leprechauns persevered, until by the end of the week the Rat showed signs of being much the best goalkeeper the Blessington Beagles had ever had. "You'll soon be playing for Ireland!" they told him, and Whiskers (who was growing enthusiastic by this time) beamed with joy.

When the day of the big match dawned hundreds of Kildare leprechauns swarmed in from places as far apart as Athy and Naas and Monasterevin; while the Blessington supporters, not to be outdone, rallied every leprechaun in the Wicklow Mountains to come down and urge their team to victory. For the first time, while he lay in his hole taking deep breaths (as his trainer had advised) and listening to the tramp of feet going by, the Rat began to feel nervous. How dreadful, he thought, if I muff the catches and make them lose the game! How awful if I fall on my face the way I did on Wednesday! But how indescribably appalling if my breeches should split and the spectators see my tail!

Once on the field, however, Whiskers had no time to think of himself: he was too busy stopping the rushes of the Punchestown forwards and keeping the ball in play. At first a group of vulgar young leprechauns gathered behind the goal-net and made great fun of him. "See the big fat goalie!" they giggled, poking one another. "Look at his hairy chest—and the length of his whiskers! He must be a quare old one—I wonder where the Beagles dug him up?" But when the game started and they saw how magnificently Whiskers could play the young leprechauns jeered no more, but stood with mouths agape as the Rat saved goal after goal, to the tumultuous applause of the mountainy men from Wicklow.

Half-time came; then twenty minutes of the second half passed, still without any score, and the Punchestown Warriors, who had looked for an easy victory, began to get rattled. In their anxiety to score they took chances; they pressed hard into the Blessington half of the pitch, leaving their defences open—so that when the Rat, with a stupendous kick, sent the ball to the Blessington captain lying well up the field, all that the Blessington player had to do was swerve past one startled back and punt the ball over the goalie's head, straight into the net. The Wicklow men went wild with excitement: they could scarcely wait for the final whistle to blow till they poured on to the field, yelling themselves hoarse as they carried their team in triumph to the pavilion.

They were all set to have a great feast there when the Rat whispered to the captain of his team and begged to be excused. The leather breeches the leprechauns had made for him were hot and tight, and his tail was aching so much after having been curled up all afternoon that Whiskers' one desire was to get rid of the cumbersome garment and be a Rat again. The captain agreed at once to let him go, since he felt that the Rat had stolen too much of the limelight already; so the Blessington Beagles celebrated their victory without their star goalie, who set out for home.

Now, just at the turnstile to the field a little man was waiting for Whiskers. He wore the Kildare colours, and the Rat would have passed him by if the stranger had not hailed him and come over with hand outstretched.

"Congratulations!" he cried. "A grand match, and you're a wonderful player—as good as many an international!"

"Thanks. Nice of you to say so," murmured the Rat, edging off.

"I see you're in a hurry," the little man remarked, "so I'll come along with you, for I want to have a chat. First of all, do you know who I am?"

"Can't say I do," admitted the Rat, as they walked along together.

"I'm the manager of the Punchestown Warriors," said the other, "and we want to make you an offer. If you'll change your residence to County Kildare and come and play on our team you can name any sum you like, and we'll give it to you. How's that for generosity?"

"Nothing doing," said the Rat.

"But you haven't taken time to consider," persisted the little man. "You'd make your reputation with us— we have a far better team, as you know—and we'll pay you well into the bargain. Won't you think it over?"

"You can't buy me," said the Rat, "because I don't play for money. I play for the honour of Wicklow."

"I see," said the little man, in a voice heavy with disappointment. "This is the very first time I've met a leprechaun who couldn't be tempted with money. You're an odd kind of leprechaun, I'm thinking, a very queer leprechaun indeed." And he stared very hard at Whiskers.

Agitated by the scrutiny, Whiskers began unwittingly to hurry, but do what he might he could not shake off the irksome company of the leprechaun from Kildare. Every step Whiskers took pained him more, until at last he could stand it no longer but wheeled angrily upon the little man.

"Go away!" cried Whiskers, making an ugly face at him. "I've told you I won't join your team, so please stop following me, or I'll call a police-dog."

"Dear me!" smiled the leprechaun. "Rude, aren't we? But what else could I expect from one of the Blessington Beagles! You needn't worry, Mr Goalie, I shan't force my company on you a moment longer." And the manager of the Punchestown Warriors turned and went back the way he had come.

The Rat plodded on round the bend of the road, and when he was quite sure he was alone he sat down and took off the breeches. Oh, what a relief it was—though he nearly wept with the pain as he straightened out the kinks in his poor cramped tail! Soon he was on his way again, carrying the breeches bundled under his arm.

But the Rat's action had not gone unobserved, as he thought. The Kildare leprechaun, his suspicions already awakened, had come stealing back to the corner and witnessed the whole performance; then, boiling with indignation, he made full speed to his headquarters at Punchestown to reveal what he had found out about the Blessington goalie—and the Punchestown Warriors planned their revenge.

A month later, when the Blessington Beagles went into Kildare to play the return match, they were in high fettle, having the Rat with them again. Rumour ran that the Punchestown team had got a new goalkeeper too, but the Beagles paid little attention to that, since they were sure nobody else could possibly be as good as

Whiskers. You can judge of their indignation when they saw stepping on to the field as fifteenth man—a Goat! Before long the boos of derision which rose from the Wicklow side of the ground gave way to hoots and yells, for every time the Blessington forwards pressed beyond their opponents' quarter-line the Goat simply sat down and blocked the goal-mouth entirely. Nobody on the Blessington side had the remotest chance of scoring so long as he was there. Trembling with anger, the manager of the Blessington team went in search of the manager of the Punchestown Warriors.

"Look here," he cried; "this is an outrage! Take that Goat off the field, and let's get on with the match."

"Ah, but he's our new goalie," smiled the Kildare man.

"I tell you the thing's absurd," shouted the Blessington leprechaun, losing his temper. "He's not a leprechaun, to begin with."

"In my little book of rules it doesn't say that all the players must be leprechauns," returned the Punchestown manager, with an impudent grin. "Would you care to consult it?"

The Wicklow man ground his teeth in rage, then he managed to splutter out, "It's not fair—not fair! Sure, that Goat's bigger than our whole team put together."

"Really?" remarked the other suavely. "I'm afraid my book of rules doesn't mention anything about the size of the players."

"It's a wonder you didn't think of sending to the Dublin Zoo for a few lions and tigers," sneered the Blessington manager sarcastically, "or maybe an odd elephant or two to bolster up your team."

"I dare say it will come to that in the end," replied the other. "Once these things begin——"

"Then the match is off!" shouted the infuriated Wicklow man.

"Splendid!" cried the Punchestown manager. "If you call it off that gives us the victory; and, according to my book of rules, you'll be suspended for six months in addition for refusing to play."

"Don't be so sure about that," bawled the Wicklow leprechaun, shaking his fist in the other's face. "Just you wait till I've lodged my complaint with the Central Council, and see who's suspended then!"

"I'd think twice before going to the Central Council if I were you," remarked the Punchestown manager, with a meaning lift of the eyebrow. "The Blessington Beagles might find themselves involved in more trouble than they bargained for, over this little matter of a goalkeeper. My suggestion would be that we get together and draw up a new set of rules—leprechaun rules. It seems that human rules leave too many loopholes for twisty leprechauns to wriggle through. What do you say?"

Realizing that he was beaten (since Whiskers' identity must have leaked out somehow), the Blessington manager grudgingly gave his assent. "Then how about to-day's match?" he growled. "Our teams can't stand there waiting till we concoct a new set of rules."

"Hardly," smiled the Kildare man, "but that's easily settled, you know. All we have to do is withdraw the two goalkeepers, substitute other players, and let the match go on. Agreed?"

The leader of the Beagles frowned and nodded, and together the two leprechauns made their way back to the field to give their decision. Whiskers and the Goat were ordered off, their places taken by leprechauns, the referee blew his whistle, and the game continued.

For Whiskers, watching from the sideline, it was gall and bitterness to see goal after goal shoot into the Blessington net—balls that he knew he could easily have stopped.

The Goat, on the other hand, was quite indifferent to the progress of the game. Having done all he was told, he was now too busy pulling pieces off the hedge even to glance at what was going on. Whiskers regarded him balefully.

He chased Whiskers all the way home

"If our team is beaten it's all your fault," he cried. "We had a great game the last time, and then you had to go and spoil everything!"

"Who cheated first?" inquired the Goat, between mouthfuls.

"You did," said Whiskers. "I could have passed as a leprechaun, but you never could. You've ruined my career. I would have been playing for Ireland next year if it wasn't for you, you interfering spoil-sport!"

Just then cheers from the Punchestown supporters indicated that a sixth goal had been scored by their side, and the Rat, mad with anger and frustration, turned and bit the Goat. Well, what could any self-respecting goat do but tear after him with lowered head and thundering hoofs? It was fortunate for Whiskers that he had remembered to take off his leather breeches before he started, or the Goat would soon have caught up with him and tossed him over the hedge. As it was, he chased Whiskers all the way home, and even after the Rat had bolted into his hole the Goat watched for a considerable time in the hope of catching him coming out.

Since that day there has been very bad feeling between them: in fact, the Rat cannot abide any place where the Goat is to be found, and makes a point of leaving as promptly as he can. Poor Whiskers! He has never quite managed to settle down to humdrum life again after his brief interlude of fame as the brilliant goalkeeper of the Blessington Beagles. Indeed, if ever you meet Whiskers coming down between the ridges of a potato field or scuffling through the leaves in a dry ditch you cannot fail to notice the disappointed expression that he wears. Whenever there's a big match on you won't see the Rat anywhere at all, because he'll be hidden at the bottom of his hole with his little hands held over his ears to shut out the sounds. And wouldn't you feel just as badly about it yourself, if you had nearly been chosen to play for Ireland and then lost your chance for ever, the way Whiskers did?

12

The Kitten's Garden

There once was a Pussy-cat called Smoky who lived near Orlock Head in the County Down. She was a little grey Cat, not quite full-grown, just the colour of a wisp of turf-smoke rising from a cottage chimney, with eyes as green as agate. Behind the house stretched a garden which Smoky loved. It was no ordinary garden, this, for sticking up through the lawn was an outcrop of bare rock that showed as plainly as a monk's tonsure; and for all that Smoky's mistress had tried to camouflage it as a rockery by planting mosses in the depressions, it still remained an obstinate, undisguisable chunk of old Silurian that had chosen to rear its head in the middle of a garden instead of decently waiting till it got to the field beyond. Yet Smoky, odd little Cat, liked that part of the garden best of all. Her favourite walk was down through the rose-arbour under the trees, along by the hawthorn-hedge at the bottom (whence she could spy solemn-faced young bullocks who stared back at her, swishing their tails), then up by the flower-border, pausing from time to time to stand on tiptoe and sniff delicately at a fragrant bloom. After her tour of inspection Smoky would spring up on the rockery, find a soft cushion of moss where the rock billowed up around her to shelter her from the breeze, and lie there basking contentedly in the sunshine. She was a very happy Cat.

One day there arrived at Smoky's house a prosperous

Dog called Bouncer. He came in a car with some visitors from the city. He was smooth and neat and groomed to a dazzling whiteness, and from the moment he jumped out on to the gravel and shook himself he behaved as though he owned the place. Though secretly a little overawed by a Dog so self-assured, Smoky remembered her manners, and once his friends had gone into the house she approached him and inquired politely, "Would you care to go round the garden?"

"Don't mind if I do," returned Bouncer indifferently. "It'll help to put in the time, I suppose. Seems a small place, I must say," he commented as they started off, with Smoky leading the way.

"Oh, but it's lovely!" breathed Smoky. "Just wait till you see!"

First she brought him into the rose-arbour. The air was sweet with the scent of the roses and the Kitten's nostrils twitched delightedly as she followed the trellised walk.

"Huh!" grunted Bouncer, looking round him. "Nothing here but ramblers and a few of the commonest varieties. You want to visit a *real* rose-garden, you know. Take ours, for example, at the end of the Malone Road—there you'd get an eye-opener! At present we're experimenting to produce a blue rose."

"How horrible!" gasped Smoky involuntarily.

"Eh? What's that?" cried Bouncer, in surprise. "It will bring in a tidy sum of money, you know, if we're successful—a very nice little packet indeed." He appeared to smack his lips in anticipation.

"I rather think I prefer my roses pink," Smoky whispered.

But Bouncer was not listening; he was standing at the first gap in the hedge, glowering through it at the bullocks in the field.

"Why haven't you had this stopped up?" he demanded, pointing with his paw to the hole in the hedge. "It's ridiculous that these—these low creatures should be able to come and gaze into anyone's private property whenever they like. Before I'd have that I'd put up a corrugated-iron fence. Look how that black bullock is staring at us! Makes it very common, you know."

"I don't mind them," smiled the Kitten. "They're all friends of mine, but he's a special friend. His name is Punch."

"Well, I never!" ejaculated Bouncer. "Perhaps it's different in the country, where you all live so close to the soil, but I know in the sphere in which I move they would definitely be said to belong to the labouring classes. It's all a question of standing on one's dignity," he continued, as he moved along the path with a grave and haughty air. "They have their place, and we have ours."

"But they never leave their place," Smoky insisted, running after him to explain. "They stay out in the field always; they never come into the garden."

Bouncer gave her a sidelong glance of disapproval. "You're a very argumentative Cat," he remarked.

Smoky was silent for a little while after that, afraid she had committed the unpardonable sin of being rude to a visitor.

"What's this muddle?" said Bouncer, stopping next before a small square patch in one corner, where twice as many flowers grew as there was room for.

"That? Oh, that's my own little garden," confessed Smoky timidly. "This is where all the animal flowers grow."

"What do you mean, 'animal flowers'?" demanded Bouncer, in his abrupt way.

"Flowers that have been called after animals," Smoky explained. Then, thinking to please him, she went on, "Look, here are some dog-daisies, and you may notice the dog-roses, too, in the hedge at the back. Aren't they pretty?"

As Bouncer did not answer, Smoky continued to enumerate her treasures. "These are shoots of pussy-willow," she said. "Of course, you should really have seen them in the spring! And next to that I have hare-bells and cowslips and cat-mint——"

"Absurd colloquial names!" sniffed Bouncer.

"Then there's cat's-ear and goat's-beard——" the Cat resumed.

"Dandelions!" interrupted Bouncer contemptuously. "Weeds, the whole lot of them—should be dug up and burnt!"

"But I just grow the things I like," said Smoky. "Whether people call them weeds or not, it makes no difference to me so long as they're pretty."

Bouncer made to turn away, showing plainly by his attitude that he considered it a waste of time talking to such a half-witted Cat; and what should Smoky do then, but call him back to admire the foxgloves that grew in her garden!

"See how big they are!" she cried ecstatically. "I can put my paw into every flower the whole way up!"

"Very interesting, I'm sure," remarked Bouncer, though his tone belied his words.

"I'm sure your paw would fit into some of the bigger blooms near the bottom of the stalk," she offered, bending the foxglove towards him encouragingly.

"I dare say," Bouncer answered, but he stood firmly on his four white paws, not in the least forthcoming.

Smoky sighed and let the foxglove swing back into place. She found her visitor heavy going, but she still tried her best to be sociable.

"What's your favourite flower?" she inquired.

"I like the rarer types of orchid," said Bouncer promptly. "The kind that run to twelve-and-sixpence for a buttonhole."

"I'll show you the flower I like best," said Smoky. "It's this dainty little blue one almost hidden among the leaves. Can you see? The country folk have a lovely name for it—they call it 'kitten's-eye-under-the-bed.' Isn't that lovely?"

"How ridiculous!" said Bouncer. "It's only a common speedwell, of no value or interest whatever."

He stalked on past the flower-border, eyeing it contemptuously.

"Come and look at the rockery," Smoky invited, making a last effort to entertain him. She indicated a narrow flagged path that twisted unevenly across the lawn.

"Why is this path not straight?" Bouncer demanded at once.

"I don't know," said the Kitten. "Why should it be? A twisty path is far more interesting than a straight one."

"But surely," Bouncer explained patiently, "the purpose of a path is to lead the pedestrian from one place to another in the shortest possible time—and here we are stupidly walking twice as far as we need."

"When I'm in a hurry I usually run across the grass," said Smoky, with an innocent air.

"Then why have a path at all?" asked the Dog. "No wonder they call this stuff 'crazy-paving'! By the way, you'll need to do something about your lawn. Look at

L

it—smothered in daisies! Remind me to give you the name of a good weed-killer before I go."

"To kill the daisies?" shrieked Smoky, appalled. "But my mistress and I, we *love* the daisies. We'd be bitterly disappointed if there were no daisies in the grass."

Bouncer cast his eyes to heaven and sighed. Clearly he thought he had strayed into a lunatic asylum. He was more than ever sure of it when Smoky proudly conducted him up the rockery.

"But it's not a rockery at all," protested the Dog, momentarily baffled. "It's only a natural outcrop of rock."

"Exactly!" smiled the Kitten. "That's what makes it so attractive."

"I'll tell you what ought to have been done at the beginning," stated Bouncer, recovering himself. "The whole rock should have been blown up with a charge of dynamite, and the pieces reset to form a proper rockery. It's too late now, though, with your house being so close. (That's the worst of these small properties.) However, that's the only way you could ever put the place right."

"And then," said Smoky, "our beautiful, uncommon rockery would be just the same as everybody else's! I shouldn't like that at all."

"It would be correct," Bouncer maintained.

Smoky sighed. "I've shown you everything now," she said. "Would you like to sit down and have a rest? Here's a good place." She prodded a mound of moss with her paw to prove how springy it was.

Bouncer glanced out of the corner of his eye at the mossy patch. "No, thanks," he said. "It's probably damp. If you'll excuse me, I'll just go and sit in the car.

I've an interior-sprung cushion there, all to myself. You've no idea how comfortable it is, and quite the latest thing."

So Smoky settled down in the rockery, while Bouncer stalked over to the car and pushed in by a door which had been left open for his convenience.

When his friends came out of the house half an hour later Smoky ran along to the end of the lane and scrambled on to the bank so that she could wave good-bye to the visitors as they drove past. But they were all talking and laughing so hard that nobody noticed the little grey Cat; and as for Bouncer (who was seated on her side of the car), he simply looked right through her and made no sign of recognition whatsoever.

Smoky felt humiliated and so resentful that she went straight to her own patch of garden and set to work on the dog-daisies, furiously tearing them up with her sharp little claws.

"I say, Smoky," came the slow, deep voice of Punch from the other side of the hedge, "don't do that. Why dig up your pretty flowers?"

"Because—because they remind me of that detestable Dog who was here all afternoon," said Smoky, with a sob.

"But the flowers can't help what the Dog said," Punch pointed out. "Call them by their other name, Smoky—ox-eye daisies, after me. You wouldn't want to destroy *my* flowers, would you?"

"Indeed, Punch, I couldn't bear to hurt your feelings," said Smoky, immediately contrite. "I never thought of that. I'm being very silly. Look, I'll push them back into the soil and they'll be none the worse." And she did so, patting the earth into place with her dainty soft paws.

Munching tranquilly, Punch watched her, and as she worked Smoky told him all about Bouncer, the critic, who wanted blue roses and a corrugated-iron fence and straight paths and no daisies on the lawn and an organized rockery; and Punch shook his huge head and made sympathetic, sighing noises until she had got the whole story off her mind and felt better.

"He's plain ignorant," concluded Punch, "that's what he is."

"Oh, no!" protested Smoky, trying to judge fairly. "He seemed a very well-educated Dog. It's just that he wanted everything different from what we're used to, and despised us for liking the simple things. He found fault with everything."

"Personally, I don't see how any place could be nicer than this—not even his garden up the Malone Road," Punch remarked, as he contemplated the landscape with a feeling of deep complacency. "Do you, Smoky?"

Smoky's gaze followed his out across the garden bright with blossom, past the rich meadow-land beyond, to where a gleam of blue sea in the distance twinkled enticingly through a fringe of trees.

"It's paradise!" agreed the little Cat, quite cheered up again. "We couldn't both be wrong and that Dog right, could we, Punch?"

"I shouldn't think it at all likely," said Punch, bending his head to wrench up a mouthful of sweet clover. As he moved away, Smoky heard him give a loud, derisive snort. "Blue roses, indeed!" said Punch.

13

The Ten-toed Monster

~~~~~~

Once upon a time the Rabbit had to go on a journey, so
he left his eldest son Bobtail in charge. Bobtail took his
responsibilities very seriously, and on the second day
after his father's departure he was out patrolling the
beach at sunrise when what should he see along the sand
but the tracks of a ten-toed monster! He gave a start of
alarm and his fur rose all along his spine and up the back
of his neck, but he was a plucky little rabbit and did not
flinch; nose to the ground, he followed those tracks on
the firm, damp sand until they led into the sea.

A dragon, said Bobtail to himself. A monster of the
deep!

Shivering with excitement, he sat down and gazed at
the tossing waves, half expecting the waters to part and
reveal the grotesque head of the unknown beast that had
walked across the bay under cover of darkness; but by
and by, as the waves kept on bouncing and tossing and
spilling into seething ripples at his feet and the day
brightened and nothing else happened, Bobtail decided
that he might as well go off duty. Yet another shock
awaited him, for when he reached the far end of the bay
didn't he spy the selfsame tracks, only this time they
were coming *out* of the sea and leading inland! The
marks were quite fresh and clear to be seen, and it was
as plain to Bobtail as his paws before him that the ten-
toed monster had come out of the water, crossed the

stretch of sand, and was now heading up the glen, bent on such ravage and destruction as the rabbit dared not contemplate. However could he warn the other animals in time?

Bobtail did not know what to do, so, like any other youngster in a predicament, he dashed off home to tell his mother all about it. Katie Rabbit received the news of his discovery very calmly—as, indeed, she took all alarms and excursions—and it was plain that she thought Bobtail's lively imagination had run away with him; but after she had fed her babies and tidied up the burrow she yielded to his pleadings and went with him to the shore. The tracks were almost obliterated now, as the sand had dried and there was a stiff breeze blowing, yet sufficient remained, if not to excite her, at least to convince her that something very peculiar had indeed walked across the beach in the early hours.

"Oh, dear," she sighed, "it would happen when your father's away!"

"What's wrong with me?" Bobtail demanded indignantly. "Can't I protect ya? I know what I'll do, I'll gather a whole pile of stones and I'll hide behind them and wait for the monster to come back to the sea, and then, my word, I'll let fly and scare the wits outa him!"

"I don't think that would solve the problem, dear," said Katie. "Nobody's ever been frightened by a rabbit: it's no use pretending. If we could only find out what exactly the creature is. . . . Only, suppose it turned out to be one of the animals we know—then wouldn't we look foolish if we had gone round spreading the news of a monster!"

"But it *is* a monster!" Bobtail insisted. "Oh, I know the tracks aren't very big, but it must be a monster. Sure, none of the animals we know hasn't got ten toeses."

"Have," his mother corrected him.

"Hasn't," Bobtail repeated.

"I'm talking about your grammar, dear," said Katie.

"Bother grammar!" Bobtail retorted. "I'm talking about toeses, which is more important. Even human beings haven't got more than five toeses on a foot, and if it was possible for them to have any more of anything they would."

"It might be an animal we haven't thought of," Katie reflected.

"Tell you what, Mum," cried Bobtail, "let's call in all the animals to-night and make them count their toeses, eh? Not the ones with hoofs or trotters, just the ones with pads. What d'ya say?"

"As you like, dear," his mother murmured, starting back up the beach. She had lost interest in the monster already, being far more concerned about the welfare of her family left in the care of her eldest daughter Fancy, who, though a helpful young rabbit, had little control over the younger bunnies and could not for long prevent them from getting into mischief. When Katie stopped at the head of the beach and looked round for Bobtail he had disappeared, but in a little while she heard him up the hill, shouting to the Badger and the Fox. Ah, well, she said to herself, it'll give him something to occupy his mind till his father comes home.

Although several of the animals were dubious when they heard the tale of an unseen, unknown monster they agreed nevertheless to meet in force that night at the end of the bay, in an unfrequented spot near the Brabla Burn, there to await the advent of Bobtail's fabled sea-dragon. When he had got them all assembled Bobtail took it upon himself to go round and count their toes. The Cow and Horse and Goat and Sheep sat aloof during this part of the proceedings, in which they were not involved. The Rat and Mouse were also dismissed, as their tracks were too small to be considered, while the Pig sat with folded trotters, chuckling with amusement at the whole affair.

"How many?" said Bobtail to the Badger.

"Five," Brock replied, stretching out his forefoot.

"Five," said the Dog.

"Five," echoed the Cat, "with a sharp claw on each."

"Five at the front and four at the back," said the Fox.

There were murmurs of disbelief as the other animals craned their necks to look, but when Bobtail counted sure enough Ruairi Fox was right, and then it was his turn to sneer!

Bobtail hurried on to the next animal. "Yes, Spike— how many toeses?"

"Five," answered the Hedgehog.

"Five," barked the Otter.

"Five," echoed the Stoat.

Then Bobtail came to his cousin, Flick the Hare, and Flick, who had been busily counting all this time, over and over again, and had got himself into quite a muddle, looked up and announced, "Six!"

"Don't be ridiculous, Flick," said Bobtail impatiently. "Hares is the same as rabbits. You can't count."

Seizing Flick's back leg, Bobtail began to count for himself. "One—two—keep still, can't you?"

"Oo-o-oh!" cried Flick. "Ee-e-eh, Bobtail, stop it— you're tickling. S-s-stop it!"

The Hare lay on his back, jerking about with hysterical squeals of laughter, while Bobtail relentlessly counted his toes on all his four feet.

"Five and five and five and five," declared Bobtail at last, hot and triumphant. "There. I told you."

"Hush!" said the Horse suddenly, raising his hoof
for silence. "Listen. There's something coming."

The animals held their breath to listen. Clearly
through the night air came the thudding sound of a beast
approaching at the gallop; above the heavy, scuttling
run they could hear its laboured breathing.

"It's running along the road, afraid of nothing,"
whispered the little Mouse, all a-tremble. "It must be
the monster!"

"Do you think it has scented us?" quavered the
Sheep. "It's coming straight here."

Instinctively the animals shrank back into a huddle.
The suspense of waiting proved too much for some of
them: the Fox broke for cover; Flick ran crazily up the
hillside; without a sound the Otter slid into the Brabla
Burn.

Thud, thud, thud! went the feet, and *huh, huh, huh!*
panted the breath, as the unknown animal came nearer.
Then the sounds changed: it was making its way
through the bracken now; it had reached the shore; after
a momentary stop to get its bearings there came the
fluffing sound of something running through loose sand.

"Is it going back into the sea?" whispered the Sheep.

Cautiously Bobtail raised his head to look. His long
ears quivered. Then he uttered a great "Whew!" and
called, "Brock, where are you? Brock! Just look who's
here!"

The Badger shouldered his way to the front and
looked in the direction Bobtail indicated. Pounding
towards them across the sand were two young badgers.
It was they who had been making the heavy running
sound; they gasped and panted with exertion, but still
they managed to summon up enough breath to call out,
"Hi ya, Bobtail Rabbit! Are we late?"

"Well, I never!" cried Brock indignantly, coming out into the open. "If it isn't my two grandchildren, Benjie and Bess! I'd like to know what they're doing at this time of night half a mile from home."

With a purposeful glint in his eye he shambled off through the sand to intercept them. The two young badgers scuffled to a halt and clutched each other. "Gee! Grandpop!" said Bess.

"False alarm, folks!" called Bobtail, before lolloping after Brock. Danger past, the other animals relaxed and began to talk quietly among themselves.

"And what's the meaning of this exhibition?" Brock was saying sternly, as he took the young badgers by the shoulders and shook them severely. "You two should be asleep in your beds. What are you doing so far from your sett?"

"We heard there was an animal party," explained Benjie, hanging his head.

"And we did so want to be there," Bess added, giving her grandfather a melting look.

"Party, indeed!" snorted Brock. "You think of nothing but amusing yourselves. It was an important animal conference, let me tell you, and if your presence had been required—a most unlikely event—you would have been invited in the usual manner. Isn't that so, Bobtail?"

"He isn't any older than we are, Grandpa," Benjie complained, in injured tones.

" 'Snot fair!" moaned Bess.

"Now, look here," Brock scolded, "I've had about enough of your pranks, you two. Foolhardy and disobedient, that's what you are; it's time you had a lesson. You needn't pout, Bess. Surely you're old enough to realize that I'm concerned for your safety when I find you wandering about by yourselves half a mile from home? You don't understand the dangers you're running into. Anything might happen to you. Have you done this kind of thing before? Answer me—have you?"

"Yes, Grandpapa," Benjie replied resignedly.

"Only once," put in Bess, "and nothing happened."

Her grandfather crushed her with a glance and addressed himself to her brother.

"How did you come—by the Knocknacarry road?"

"Yes, Grandpa," answered Benjie.

"It's a wonder a motor-car didn't knock you down," Brock grunted. "And then across the bridge, I suppose?"

Benjie nodded.

"And through the village?"

Benjie nodded again, looking more crestfallen every minute.

"Of all the crazy things to do!" cried Brock. "I'll speak to your mother about this and have you two kept under stricter supervision in future. Be off home with you at once, you rogues, before I really lose my temper!"

Benjie turned obediently and began to run up the beach. Bess hesitated, gazed reproachfully at her grandfather, and then veered off after her brother, and was soon following in his tracks, the way she always did.

"Go back across the fields now!" shouted Brock after their retreating figures. "No more races along the road!"

"Yes, Grandpapa," came Benjie's voice, faint on the wind.

The Badger was just about to follow Bobtail back to where the other animals were when he stopped abruptly to stare at the sand beneath him. He took a few steps and stopped again. Then, "Bobtail," he called, in a strange voice, "have you seen this?"

Bobtail pattered over to his side. There on the beach, too plain for any argument, was a footmark which bore the imprint of ten toes!

"But—but—how did it get there?" stammered Bobtail. "We've been here for ages, and nobody's passed this way."

"Can't you guess?" smiled Brock. "When Benjie runs Bess always follows a yard or two behind him. It must happen sometimes that their tracks coincide; that's what has happened here, hence the track of ten toes instead of five. Look, over here the tracks have separated—you can tell quite clearly that there were two animals running along—but farther on they merge again. In fact, it looks as if we've solved the mystery of your monster, Bobtail!"

"But the tracks I saw came out of the sea," said Bobtail, still mystified.

"Because the tide had washed over them," Brock explained. "They appeared to lead into the sea and out of it again, but they didn't really—they just went straight across the beach."

"Oh, dear!" sighed Bobtail, unable to deny the evidence. "You mean there's no monster?"

"Why, aren't you glad?" said Brock, surprised. "I thought you'd be delighted. What's the matter, Bobtail?"

"Nothing much, I suppose," said Bobtail dismally, "except that I'm going to look a queer fool when the other animals find out that there never was any monster at all, but only a couple of young badgers. Are you going to tell them, Brock?"

"Come, now," said Brock cheerfully. "It isn't such a serious matter as all that, surely? You're not the first animal to make a mistake, you know. No harm's done, so why worry?"

"But they'll all laugh at me," wailed Bobtail, "and I couldn't bear it if they laughed, especially the Fox. I'd sooner run away. Before my father went on his travels he put me in charge of everything and told me to be on guard and always to be watchful, and I was doing my best when——"

"Bless you, Bobtail, that's all right!" Brock interrupted. "I see how you're fixed, and they'll not get a word out of me, any of them; you can depend on that, so set your mind at ease. But have you considered how you're going to explain the disappearance of the monster?"

"That's easy," replied Bobtail, perking up at once. "I'll charm it away. No, I have a better idea—I'll send it a message in a bottle."

"In a bottle?" queried Brock.

"Yes," said Bobtail, "and cast it out to sea."

"Well, well," smiled the Badger, "you do think of the things!" He accompanied Bobtail to see how his plan would work, and was secretly much amused by the speed with which the plausible little rabbit convinced the other animals that this was the one and only way to get rid of a monster. No less a creature than the Wise Salmon had told him so. They were all eager to co-operate: in next to no time the Otter had fetched up a bottle he knew about lying in the bed of the stream, the Rat produced a fairly clean piece of paper, and Bobtail sent home to his burrow for his thick blue pencil. Then he carefully inscribed the message in these words:

DEAR MONSTER
    You would be far better off at Rathlin Island. Take our advice.
    [signed] THE ANIMALS OF CUSHENDUN
                      (per B. Rabbit)

"Why Rathlin?" inquired the Sheep, with a worried expression. (She had relatives there.)

"Just because it's the farthest-away place I can think

*The way he came pounding down the beach with
head bent made everybody shrink*

of," Bobtail replied, pushing the cork in firmly with his paw. "Can anybody throw?"

"I'll swim out with it," offered the Dog.

"Oh, no," cried the Mouse, "you mustn't think of it. The monster might catch you."

"I'll butt it for you if you like," the Goat suggested. "I can butt things a long way."

"Don't let him," said the Rat. "He'll break it."

"I know what," said Bobtail, "I'll wrap it up in sea-weed so it won't break, and I'll set it on a sand-castle (we can soon make one), and then the Goat can take a running leap at it and launch it through the air the way he said. After that the tide will carry it out to the monster's home. What d'ya say, folks?"

Already willing paws were scraping the sand together and the Goat was measuring his paces up the beach. His take-off was magnificent, and the way he came pounding down the beach with head bent made everybody shrink. Sand flew in all directions as he cannonaded into the sand-castle, and the next thing the animals could see was the bottle with its streamers of seaweed rising high in the air, describing a graceful curve, and descending into the sea some twenty yards out. The *plop* as it struck the water could be distinctly heard. A united cheer rose from the beach, and as Bobtail watched the bottle bobbing on the crest of the waves, going farther and farther out on the retreating tide, he rubbed his paws together and beamed with satisfaction. Perhaps it was his smug expression that annoyed the Fox, for suddenly Ruairi was heard to remark, "I wonder if there ever was any monster at all—outside Bobtail's imagination, I mean?"

Before Bobtail could give vent to an indignant reply Brock intervened. "I saw the tracks myself," he said. "I'll bear witness to that."

"Indeed?" said the Fox. "What a pity you didn't think of calling on any of the rest of us to have a look!"

"We could have," came Bobtail's quick answer, "only

you weren't there. You ran for your life when you heard the monster coming. Remember?"

Some of the other animals chuckled, and the Fox stiffened with anger. "Anyhow," he added, as a parting shot, "I don't think much of your remedy. Whoever heard of a monster taking himself off because he got a message in a bottle? It's absurd."

"Wait and see, Ruairi," said Brock evenly. "Time will tell."

And since Brock made sure that the young badgers stayed up in the hills after that, even the Fox was forced to admit in the end that Bobtail's plan must have worked, for the tracks of the ten-toed monster were never seen on Cushendun beach again.

Leabarlanna Puibliḋe
Catraċ Áta Cliat

/ Libraries

D

Withdrawn From Stock